Secret Lovers With Their…

DARK
YEARNINGS

On Newsstands Now:

TRUE STORY
and
TRUE CONFESSIONS
Magazines

True Story and *True Confessions* are the world's largest and best-selling women's romance magazines. They offer true-to-life stories to which women can relate.

Since 1919, the iconic *True Story* has been an extraordinary publication. The magazine gets its inspiration from the hearts and minds of women, and touches on those things in life that a woman holds close to her heart, like love, loss, family and friendship.

True Confessions, a cherished classic first published in 1922, looks into women's souls and reveals their deepest secrets.

To subscribe, please visit our website:
www.TrueRenditionsLLC.com or call **(212) 922-9244**

To find the TRUES at your local store, please visit:
www.WheresMyMagazine.com

Secret Lovers With Their…

DARK YEARNINGS

From the Editors
Of *True Story* And
True Confessions

Published by True Renditions, LLC

True Renditions, LLC
105 E. 34th Street, Suite 141
New York, NY 10016

ISBN: 978-1-938877-90-2

Visit us on the web at www.truerenditionsllc.com.

Contents

MORE THAN
JUST FRIENDS
I Wanted Him—Body And Soul!

Jonathan looked down at me with his big brown eyes, a smile quirking those full, luscious lips. My heart did a quick tumble before I was able to recover, which I had to do to answer his question. And I had to answer because Jonathan and I were friends and I wasn't about to let him think I was mad at him for any reason.

"No, I don't have a date for the Main Street Ball," I told him. "I was supposed to go with Anthony, but he has finals and he's staying at school that weekend."

"I don't have a date, either," he said as his smile faded. "Why don't you and I just get dressed up and go together?" He paused before adding, "After all, what are friends for?"

Yeah, what are friends for? One look at Jonathan was all any red-blooded girl needed to know that being "just friends" with him was impossible. He and his mom had lived next door to my family since we were in elementary school, so I wasn't supposed to think of anything romantic with him in mind. But that was impossible. As he got older, he only got better—sexier, more athletic, and definitely smarter. And of course, girls were constantly swarming around him.

With a shrug that I hoped looked more casual than I felt, I said, "I guess that would be okay."

Jonathan snickered. "Well, I know I'm only second choice, but you can at least pretend you enjoy being with me."

"Oh, Jonathan, I do enjoy being with you," I said. "It's just that..." How could I tell this man how hard it was to keep my hands off him when what I really wanted to do was wrap my arms and legs around the man and claim him for my own? I never finished my sentence because I couldn't tell him what I was really thinking.

After agreeing to go to the ball with Jonathan, we went into our respective houses. The aroma of dinner cooking wafted through the downstairs, but I felt hunger for nothing but Jonathan. I ran quickly upstairs before my mother could summons me to help set the table while she put the finishing touches on dinner. I couldn't face her with these sexy thoughts in my mind.

"All I want is to ravish his body every time I see him," I wrote. "When he licks his lips, I imagine them licking my breasts, and I almost melt from the inside out."

1

The more I wrote, the faster I went, and my thoughts tumbled onto the pages as if my life depended on getting it down in record time.

"I want him to kiss me all over and let me touch every inch of his body. Those big, dark, muscled arms are smooth as they pull me closer. As we kiss, he moans his desire and tells me how much he wants me. I tease him until he can't take it anymore, so he begs me to make love to him. After all, this is what he's been wanting since. Well, since he first laid eyes on me." This was my imagination, so I figured I might as well give in to my dreams.

"'Oh, Shawna, you're the most beautiful woman on the face of the earth," he whispers. "All I ever wanted was you." And then he slowly removes my clothes and his, making a fun striptease game out of it. I lean away, but he tugs on me because he can't stand being apart from me. He slowly separates my legs as he glides between them, calling out wonderful pet names for me. I continue to tease him until he lets me know he's going to possess me, so I'd better be ready.

"Ready is my middle name," I whisper as he glides inside me, slowly thrusting then pulling out in a fluid motion. I bite my bottom lip as he tells me how much he loves me."

The more I write, the more I want Jonathan. Shutting my eyes for a moment, I could almost feel his presence in the room.

"Shawna!" my mom called from downstairs, bursting the bubble of my journal entry that had turned into a one-act sex play. "Dinner's ready!"

I suffered a sigh. "Coming. I'll be right there," I hollered back."

My hands shook as I closed the book and carefully locked it to keep prying eyes from seeing my deepest thoughts and desires. If anyone ever saw this, they'd certainly try to use it against me. It was too hot and too juicy not to.

During dinner, I told my mom and dad that Jonathan and I were going to the Main Street Ball together. They exchanged a glance.

"What's wrong with that?" I asked.

"Nothing," Dad replied. "It's just that we know how much you wanted to go to the ball with Anthony." His voice was guarded through all his comments.

"I hope you're not too disappointed to be stuck with Jonathan," Mom added. "Just don't let him know he's your second choice."

"He already knows," I told them. "But that's okay. He understands. We're old friends, and we tell each other everything."

It took every ounce of self-restraint I had to not look them in the eye and confess all—that I was madly in love, and lust, with Jonathan. Somehow, though, it didn't seem right since he and I were such good friends. We knew each other too well, living next door to each other for all these years. We'd talked about what we liked in the opposite sex. He always laughed at me, saying I was a fairy princess and wanted a knight in shining armor to rescue me from the dragon. I turned the tables and accused him of wanting to be the knight—but only for another damsel. He didn't say anything to that and often changed the subject.

The problem was that the more I knew about Jonathan, the more I loved him. Not only was he the best-looking guy in town, he had a heart of gold, and he was sweet.

The next day, Jonathan and I chatted about the ball. He asked me what color my dress was, and I told him. The more we talked, the more I felt I risked drooling over him and making a fool of myself. As soon as I had a chance, I told him I needed to go home. I ran to my room and reread my journal entry and pined for what I feared would never be.

Mom had dinner on the table when I got downstairs. My dad had to work late, so it was just the two of us.

"I saw you talking to Jonathan. How's he been?" she asked.

I shrugged. "He's fine." I couldn't look her in the eye for fear of her seeing my true feelings, especially after what I'd just written in my journal.

"I've always thought that boy was special," Mom said. "He's bright and handsome."

"Uh huh," I mumbled as I racked my brain to think of something else to talk about. If I didn't change the subject, no telling how far Mom would go with this, and I wasn't in the mood to expose any of my feelings to her.

I started talking about my job, and she went along with it. Then she blind-sided me by asking about the Main Street Ball.

"Too bad you're not going with Anthony," she said, as if testing me. I could tell by the tone of her voice that she didn't care for Anthony. She'd once called him a player, but what she really didn't like was that he didn't match up to Jonathan.

"I know, but he won't be back in town."

"At least you're going. I'm just glad Jonathan asked you, but I must say I'm a little surprised."

"Why are you surprised?" I asked. "Since we're both single, and neither of us had a date, it was only natural. All our friends will be there. Maybe we'll even have fun together," I said, mocking her meddling.

A smile began to form on her lips. "Now, that's a great idea. One I would have thought of myself."

I quickly finished eating, carried my plate to the sink, washed it, and then excused myself to be alone. There were times when I wanted to be in my own apartment, but I still wasn't making enough at my

3

job to get a decent place, and my parents let me stay in the house rent-free so I could save my money. Still, though, I hated the interrogation about my love life.

The evening of the ball was absolutely perfect. The temperature had fallen to a comfortably cool level, there wasn't a cloud in the sky, exposing all the stars and the moon in their full glory. I sighed as I opened the door to a tuxedo-clad Jonathan who looked better than anything I'd ever seen in a magazine. The piping on his shirt matched my dress. My spirits soared. He held out a wristband corsage that matched, and said, "Here, Shawna, let me put this on you." I held out my hand while he slipped it onto my wrist.

"My, don't you two make a handsome couple," Mom said from behind me. "Have fun, kids. We won't wait up."

As Jonathan held the door of his car for me, he chuckled. "Your mom's too obvious."

"Yeah, sorry about that," I apologized.

"No problem. My mom's the same way. She doesn't understand why you and I aren't an item."

I sighed. I agreed with his mom and mine, but I didn't say a word to Jonathan about my feelings. No point in scaring him away. Being friends with him was better than completely losing him.

Jonathan found a parking spot near the entrance of the ballroom. "Wait for me, Shawna. I'll come around and get you." Such a gentleman.

As he opened the door, his eyes flashed with something I'd never noticed before. If I didn't know better, I'd think it was admiration and maybe even attraction. But I couldn't allow my hopes to take over. It would just set me up for disappointment later.

Extending his arm, he said, "Ready to face the crowd?"

"Yep," I said as I tucked my hand in the crook of his elbow. I felt the sizzle of my feelings at the slightest touch, so I tried to pull my hand back. He wouldn't let me, though. He used his other hand to hold mine in place.

I was speechless as we entered the room. All heads turned, and people grew quiet. Jonathan leaned down and whispered, "This is so stuffy. I don't want to stay long."

We quickly found some people we both knew and joined them. However, there was one woman who couldn't seem to stop staring at Jonathan.

"Don't look now, Jonathan," I whispered. "But that woman can't take her eyes off you."

He glanced over then back at me. "Who is she?"

I shrugged. "I have no idea."

Then Jonathan said, "Every guy here is looking at you, Shawna. I have a feeling you can have your pick of anyone here."

"Hmm," I teased, "where should I start? So many men, not enough time."

Jonathan nodded and pursed his lips. At first he didn't say anything but after a few seconds, he replied, "You just start with one, and when you're finished, just move on."

"Is that how you do it?" I asked. My heart was ripping from my chest, but I couldn't help but ask the question I knew would hurt.

"Of course. When you've got it, you have to use it."

We were deep in this painful discussion when an old mutual friend of ours tapped Jonathan on the shoulder and said, "My friend Angel wants to meet you." Looking at me, she winked. "Since you and Jonathan are just friends, I didn't think you'd mind."

"No," I said as a lump formed in my throat. "Of course not. Go ahead, Jonathan. The women of the world are waiting for you. Maybe this will be your lucky night."

He offered me an odd look, but then a smile quickly formed on his face. "Thanks, Shawna. You're a trooper."

That was the last I saw of Jonathan until he came up and told me he was taking Angel home. The woman who'd brought Angel had offered me a ride, and Jonathan said he figured I wouldn't mind.

Again, I gave him permission to abandon me. I hated every single thought that entered my mind at that point. I wanted to strangle everyone in the room—Angel, the woman who brought her, and Jonathan for doing this to me. I'd hoped in the back of my mind that something special would happen between us tonight, since it had started out so magical with the gorgeous sky and mood I'd had when I first opened the door when he'd come to pick me up. I glanced down at my corsage and thought, we even match for heaven's sake. Isn't that supposed to mean something?

All night, I tossed and turned in bed. I couldn't get the image of Jonathan and Angel out of my mind.

When I went downstairs to breakfast the next morning, Mom asked me how my date with Jonathan went. I told her it wasn't a date and that I'd been taken home by a friend so he could be with someone he'd met.

Clucking her tongue, Mom said, "Shawna, when will you ever learn not to be so nice to other women? He was your date last night. You have to learn to hang onto your man."

I started to argue with her, but thought better of it. I finished eating as much as I could, then I went back to my room.

As the day wore on, I'd worked myself into an emotional frenzy over the whole thing. Finally, I decided I couldn't handle it anymore. I needed to confront Jonathan and let him know how I felt. If it hurt our friendship, at this point, I didn't care. My heart had been broken in half last night, and he needed to know.

I carefully put on my makeup and fixed my hair in the most flattering style. Then I put on my low-cut red shirt that people told me was sexy on me, and I left the top button undone. After studying my reflection in the mirror, I figured I might as well go and get this over with.

Mustering all the courage I had, I left my house, crossed the yards, and walked up to his door. I knocked.

Jonathan answered it while my fist was still banging on his door.

"Whoa there, Shawna. What's going on?"

My heart was in my throat, and I wasn't sure if I was doing the right thing, but right now I didn't care. I had to do this for my sanity.

"Why did you leave me last night?" I asked in an accusing tone.

Jonathan frowned. "Did that bother you?"

I thrust my hand on my hip and glared at him. "What do you think?"

A slow grin took over his mouth, and he stepped back. "Come on in, Shawna. My mom's gone, and she won't be back until this afternoon."

I followed him inside. "You still haven't answered me."

"Okay, I'll answer you, but only after you answer my question."

"What?"

"Why did you tell me to go with her? If I remember correctly, you almost pushed me away, telling me it might be my lucky night."

I shut my eyes as I thought back over what had happened. Then my eyes sprang open. "I did, didn't I?"

He nodded but didn't say a word. He just stood there, his arms folded, staring at me. I couldn't tell what he was thinking.

"Did you?" I asked with a squeaky voice.

"Did I what?"

"Get lucky?"

Jonathan tilted his head back and let out a hearty chuckle. Then he reached out and took both of my hands. "You sound like a jealous girlfriend."

"I am," I replied sheepishly. "Maybe I'm not your girlfriend, but I'm jealous."

Again, he laughed. "You're kidding, right?"

"No, I'm not kidding. What's so funny?" I asked as my heart ached at his lighthearted response. I didn't get the humor.

"That you're jealous over me. I've been wanting to put Anthony's lights out ever since he started coming around."

"You have?" I asked as I tried to step away but was stopped by Jonathan's firm grip on my hands. "Why?"

"I don't like the thought of him putting his hands on you."

"Really?"

"Yes, I've been in love with you since we were little kids. I just kept hoping you'd fall in love with me, too. It was beginning to look like all I had was a pipe dream, and I'd never get my wish."

Suddenly, I felt like jumping his bones. But I didn't. Instead, I grinned, batted my eyelashes, and said, "Well, maybe if you're really sweet, I might be able to accommodate your most secret desires."

He blinked as he looked at me, almost as if he didn't believe what I was saying. Still holding my hands, he continued staring at me.

"Well, Jonathan?" I asked. "What'll it be? Wanna give this love thing between us a chance?" I swallowed deeply and added, "I want to make love to you, Jonathan." I knew I was in deep water, but I didn't care. It was sink or swim time, and I knew it. "And I want to do it now."

"Oh, baby," was all he said as he pulled me to his chest.

Next thing I knew, we were walking toward his bedroom, which was in the back of his house. His arm was tight around my waist, and I was holding onto him for dear life.

We were barely inside his room when he turned me around to face him. "Are you sure you want to do this?" he asked.

I nodded and began to unfasten the top button of my shirt. He gasped as more and more of my breast was exposed.

Jonathan's eyes never left my body as I did a slow, deliberate striptease for him. Then I reached out and began to remove his clothing. He stood there like a statue, until I got to his jeans. He covered my hands with his as he leaned down and kissed me, first on my eyelids then my cheeks. His lips covered mine, and his tongue hungrily darted around my lips and found its way into my mouth.

We playfully nipped and fondled as we explored each other's bodies. I loved the way he felt up close. This was much better than anything I'd ever imagined. Jonathan was a wonderful lover, leaving no area untouched. My senses were all on fire as he asked me if I was ready.

As he entered my body, I moaned. He looked down at me and said, "I love you with all my heart, Shawna. This is what I've been waiting for all my life."

Nothing could have prepared me for the intoxicating feelings that flooded me as we made love. The sexual stimulation was heightened by my love for Jonathan, plus the fact that he was so tender and considerate of my feelings allowed me to be in a place I've never been. It was truly the most sensual pleasure I'd ever received.

When we both reached our peak, he hung onto me as if clinging for life. I snuggled in the crook of his body and enjoyed the scent of raw, hungry sex.

7

As he looked down into my eyes and repeated his words of love, I smiled and nestled even closer.

That day was a turning point in our lives. After that, neither of us even looked at another person. Naturally, our parents were happy. But no one was as thrilled as me.

I went back to my journal entry later—the one with the love scene I'd imagined. I couldn't help but laugh at how the real thing made my imagination look like child's play. Jonathan was oh, so much better than anything I could have dreamed. What's wonderful is he says the same thing about me.

THE END

I COULDN'T TELL HIM
MY DARK SECRET

Waylon Jones and I have been friends forever. We grew up together and eventually got jobs as teachers in the same school. And I was secretly in love with him. Only Mary, another teacher, knew. She constantly told me to tell Waylon how I felt, but I was afraid it would ruin our friendship and kept things the way they were. But, I would dream of him at night, imagining how it would be to have him love me. Until it actually happened.

Waylon and I had gone together to a colleague's wedding. He was interested in a new teacher, who seemed just as interested as him, until she walked into the wedding reception on the arm of another man.

I watched Waylon attempt to drink his cares away. I wanted to take him in my arms, kiss his hidden tears away, and tell him everything would be all right. Before he got too drunk, I managed to get him into the car and drove him home.

I tried to get him into his bedroom so I could help him undress and get into bed, but he kept grabbing at me, calling me Kendra. All at once, his lips were locked on mine. The tiny guiding voice in the back of my head told me to get him into bed and go home. But as his hands began to wander down my body, I found myself kissing him back.

Before long my dress was on the floor and Waylon was suckling a nipple and driving me crazy. I soon reached the point of no return. Since Waylon continued to think I was Kendra, I felt safe and decided to make the most of that magic moment which might never happen again.

It was a wonder Waylon could perform as well as he did. After all, he had downed a great deal of liquor. When the magic had ended, I left him in bed and went home still tingling, wishing I had remained by his side. I was still thinking about him when he called the next day.

"I had the strangest dream last night, Tracy?"

"Uh-huh."

"I dreamed I was making love to Kendra——only there were moments when she looked like you."

"Probably because I had helped you into bed," I said quickly, hoping he'd accept that explanation and move on.

"Oh, yeah, I guess. Hey, it's a gorgeous day. Want to go biking?"

"Sure, why not?"

"Great! I'll see you in a few."

I had lunch with Mary on Monday. She had seen me push Waylon out the door at the wedding reception.

"Did you get Waylon home in one piece?"

"Uh-huh."

"By that look on your face I'd say you did a lot more than that."

"We made love."

"What! Did you finally tell him?"

"No. He thought I was Kendra and it was all a dream."

"Unbelievable. You should have stayed and told him."

"No. I couldn't spoil it for him. He thought he was loving Kendra."

"But, it wasn't Kendra's body that gave him the pleasure."

"In his mind it was. I was afraid he'd see me in the morning and regret what happened."

"But what if he didn't?"

"I was too afraid to risk it."

The bell rang signaling the end of the period. The rest of the day blew by and I went home. After a quick dinner I began to grade papers when the phone rang. It was Waylon and he sounded down.

"Kendra is really seeing that other guy."

"I'm sorry, Waylon. But cheer up. You still have my love."

He chuckled. I doubt if he realized how much truth there was in what I had just said. "Listen, I don't feel like being alone tonight. Would you like some company?"

He should only know how much I desired his company—every night.

"Sure, come on over."

I wondered how many more times I would have to console him. Actually it didn't matter. I'd always be there for him. What did matter was what would I do when he finally found the woman of his dreams and got married? The possibility scared me.

Several months passed. Kendra was now engaged and Waylon seemed to be well over her. There wasn't one steady woman to upset my tranquility until Waylon met Lynette.

"Tracy! I've been looking all over for you."

"Hi, Waylon. You certainly sound cheerful this morning."

"You're not going to believe this, but I went to the grocery store last night and met the girl of my dreams down the frozen foods aisle."

"That's nice," I said, not meaning a single word.

"Yeah. Her name is Lynette. She's one fine woman."

Waylon was smitten. He and Lynette began to date. It wasn't long before he asked me to help him pick out an engagement ring for her. He felt that he was in love with her. There was nothing I could do but be happy for him. Therefore I accompanied him to the jewelry store and helped him select a ring that I wished were mine.

He intended to give her the ring the following night.

"She's going to love the ring. I know I do. The guy who goes with the ring is kinda nice also."

"Thanks, Tracy," he said, hugging me.

Waylon dropped me off at my apartment. I was so miserable that I cried myself to sleep that night.

The next morning Mary saw me in the hall. "My God! You look like hell. What did you do last night? Lose your best friend?"

"Yes. Waylon bought a ring for Lynette."

"Oh, no!"

"It's over," I said, tears filling my eyes anew.

"Why didn't you ever let him know how you feel about him?"

"You know why."

"Maybe things might have been different."

I shook my head. "I've been in front of him for years."

"Sometimes people don't see the forest for the trees. You were so close to him that you became invisible."

I looked at her wondering if she might be right in that respect.

"Tell me, what will you say to Waylon when he sees you looking like you do?"

"I don't know. I'll think of something."

"Try the truth. It will set you free."

Actually I got lucky and avoided Waylon most of the day. When I did see him, it was outside and I was wearing my sunglasses. This was good, for I couldn't come up with a decent lie, anyway.

No matter what I did that night, all I could think about was Waylon asking Lynette to marry him. When I finally fell into a fitful sleep, I was awakened by someone banging on my front door as if they wanted to break it down.

"Tracy! Wake up! I need to speak to you!"

It was Waylon. I looked at the time. It was 3:00 am. He was making such a racket, I feared that one of my neighbors would shoot him first and then call the cops. I jumped out of bed and rushed to the door. I opened it and he fell inside.

"What's wrong?"

"She's a rotten two-timing whore."

"Who?" I asked as if I couldn't figure it out.

"Lynette. Who else?"

"Didn't you go to her place tonight to ask her to marry you?"

"Yup."

"Well what happened?"

"I found her in bed with another man."

"Oops."

"That slut was seeing him the entire time."

"What did she say to you when you found her with the other man?"

"Nothing."

"You're kidding?"

"No, I'm not. I didn't wait around to hear a pack of lies. Damn that woman!" he said, sliding down the wall to the living room floor.

My heart went out to him as I joined him on the floor. I put my arms around his shoulders to comfort him. "I'm so sorry, baby, honestly I am," I said and gently rubbed his back.

"What's wrong with me? Why do I always choose women with more baggage than American Tourister?"

"I don't know. Maybe you just have a good heart and lots of band aids to cover broken wings."

He buried his head in my chest and murmured something unintelligible. My body began to react to his closeness and I was reminded of how little I was wearing. When I had rushed to the door I had forgotten that I had on a sheer negligee. Waylon had noticed the hardening of my nipples.

He lifted his head and looked at me in a way he hadn't before. Like a magnet, my lips met his. He gently kissed me and then pulled away to gaze into my eyes once more. Then he kissed me again, only with more passion this time. I kissed him back with urgency.

We were breathless when we separated once more.

"Something about kissing you feels so familiar—and so right," he said. "Have we done this before?"

I didn't answer. What would I have said? Waylon became insistent, though and demanded an answer. I had to tell him the truth.

"You got pretty trashed the night of Anne's wedding reception."

"How well I remember. I had some hangover the next morning."

"I tried to get you home before you made an idiot out of yourself. Seeing Kendra with that other guy had pushed you over the edge. Unfortunately, you didn't make things easy for me. I had a tough time getting you into the car, let alone into the apartment. When I finally got you home and tried to get you into bed, you became an octopus. I couldn't get you to stop groping me. You thought I was Kendra."

"You're kidding?"

"Not in the least."

"Wait a sec! That dream I told you about, you remember?"

I nodded.

"It wasn't a dream was it?"

"No."

"It was you, wasn't it? I made love to you, not Kendra."

"Yes."

"Why? Why did you let me?" Waylon drew me towards him. "Why, Tracy?"

"Because…because…I love you. I…always have."

He groaned. I thought he was going to rush out of there and our friendship would be over. Everything would be over. But he didn't leave.

"Why didn't you ever tell me?"

"Because I thought you wanted to remain my friend and nothing more. I was willing to accept that if I could be close to you. I was always afraid of losing your friendship."

He shook his head and groaned again. "What a colossal joke."

"What?"

"Do you have any idea how many times I wanted to take you in my arms and kiss you, desiring to cross that platonic line we had drawn between us?"

I shook my head in disbelief. "And you never did."

"No, for basically the same reasons you kept your feelings to your—we've let enough time pass through our hands."

I was unaware that tears were falling from my eyes until he began to kiss them away, one at a time. I put my hands around his neck and drew him closer to me. He covered my lips with his. "I believe this is where we left off."

He slid his lips down the side of my neck. I could feel a quickening between my thighs. My body remembered the pleasure it received the last time Waylon and I made love. A moan escaped from my throat as he lowered my nightgown and fastened his lips to a quivering breast.

A moment later, he swept me into his arms and carried me into the bedroom. I watched as he stepped out of his clothes and joined me on the bed.

"You're so beautiful," he said. "Everything a man could want in a woman. Promise me you'll never leave me." There were tears in his eyes. I couldn't believe any of this was happening. It was as if my dreams had suddenly come true.

"Waylon, I'll never leave you. I promise," I replied and then sealed the promised with a kiss.

He slowly covered me in kisses from head to toe, driving me wild with desire. Every spot on my body he touched felt aflame. I could hardly wait to feel him deep within me. A gasp of pleasure escaped my lips as he slowly entered. This was real—no fears, no guilt. I truly succumbed to the magic and found myself in heaven. Moments later, Waylon followed me there.

We fell asleep. I dreamed that I had been lost on a desert island. I would travel in circles, but could never find the boat that brought me there. Finally Waylon appeared and kissed me. Moments later I was on the boat making love to him. It felt so real. I opened my eyes and I discovered it was real—only we were on my bed.

Lucky for both of us it was Saturday. I doubt if we could have made it to school. When we finally separated from each other long enough to get out of bed and shower, we had some breakfast and talked.

There was so much we had to say to one another and so much we needed to do, as if we were trying to make up for lost time. We ended up spending much of the day in bed exploring the possibilities and each other. Finally I dressed and went with Waylon to his place where he changed so we could go out to dinner.

After we ordered, Waylon spoke. "Tracy, in the short time that we've been intimate, I've discovered something very important."

"What's that?"

"That I love you."

I smiled.

"And I love that gorgeous smile of yours—as well as the rest of you," he said, taking my hand and kissing it.

Reaching into his pocket, he pulled out a familiar-looking box. Instantly my heart began to pound against my chest. He opened it and slipped the ring on my finger. It was the engagement ring that I had selected for Lynette.

"Are you sure?"

"Never more sure of anything in my life. Will you marry me?"

"You have to ask?"

He chuckled.

"When do you want to get married?"

"As soon as we can put together a wedding. Why wait and add to our foolishness?"

On Monday morning Mary stopped me in the hall after I brought my class to lunch.

"You look beautiful, Tracy. What a difference from the other day."

"I feel beautiful," I said lifting my hand so she could see the ring.

Her eyes nearly popped out of her head. "Who and when?"

"Waylon."

"Did you sell your soul to the Devil?"

"No. It was just a little miracle."

"You better explain and don't leave a single thing out."

I told her everything. I couldn't believe how right she had been.

She shook her head in disbelief. "Two idiots. Unbelievable. But the most important thing is that everything worked out for the best— despite the both of you. I'm so happy for you. When's the wedding?"

"We haven't picked a date yet, but will you be my Matron of Honor?"

"I'd be honored and delighted. This is one wedding I wouldn't miss for all the world," she said and gave me a big hug.

THE END

HIGH SCHOOL LOVE
I Can't Seem To Forget Him!

It had been a long day and I was tired yet satisfied. The window behind me was open, the fall breeze making my hair dance on my shoulders while the scent of damp leaves poured in. I was the last one in the building. I sat, looking over one of my cases for the final time before punching the clock. I turned to steal a glance out the window and let my mind drift for a moment on how wonderful my life is.

"If you keep working these long hours, someone might begin feeling neglected," the deep voice said from behind.

I turned, smile already in full bloom, to find Juwan leaning against the inside of the jamb. Even now, his looks stole my breath. He was built rugged like his bones were made of iron and stood like he couldn't be toppled. He allowed his smile to maneuver across his thick, sensual lips.

"Well, I wouldn't want that," I said playfully. "How can I make sure that everyone feels important?"

Juwan stepped inside my office, closing the door behind him. As he did, I became acutely aware of the ripple effect a simple motion can trigger. Against his white, button down shirt, the plump plateau of his pec flexed to the surface, the sienna tone of his skin muted enticingly against the cotton. The contour of his behind pressed into the loose gabardine of his slacks, giving the slightest hint of his dimple. As he turned his head, the cords of his neck thickened and my lips tingled, growing eager to taste. Without laying a finger on me, Juwan was touching me deeper than any lover ever had.

He guided me onto the desk so that I was sitting and he was standing between my legs. The mingled scent of his cologne and his natural smell overpowered the autumnal potpourri drifting in from the open window. I breathed it in deep and held it inside of me, savoring it the way a smoker would a long drag after a tiring day.

The power of his lips startled me; they were almost electric when they found the stalk of my neck. Juwan pulled himself closer so that the hardness of his body was invading the softness of my own. Being so close to him encouraged me to let go, to allow myself to be overcome. I ran my fingertips around the back of his head, down his neck and between his shoulder blades. There, I rested my fingers, feeling his muscles work as he loosened the buttons on my blouse and drove his hot mouth across my bosom.

Juwan whispered something to me and I heard myself giggle but

15

it came to my ears from a distance like I was far below it. I was in the kind of stupor that you find when you're so intoxicated that you loose track of time and space. Replacing my thoughts was the sublime sensation of pleasure dripping through my body. It felt as if my naked body was being tickled by a thousand butterfly wings at once.

When I parted my eyes, I found the setting sun had washed the office in a surreal fuchsia. Juwan's bare shoulders glistened with stray sunlight, while his tummy was a chocolaty block of folding shadows. I became very aware of my thighs being swallowed by the grip of his massive hands then of the stone presence filling me up. I gasped, suddenly overloaded yet in wondrous bliss. Then….

"Please make sure your trays are in their up and locked position."

I woke up the way you do from dreams you don't want to end, feeling a little confused and wishing I could go back and finish. But that never happened. Outside the window, the ground was pulling up beneath us. A strange mix of excitement and fear flooded my body, causing me to shudder a little. Here I was on the doorstep of my new life. Now all I had to do was find Juwan Harper and make him fall in love with me…again.

Juwan and I had gone to high school together and somewhere between study hall and the long walks home on spring afternoons, we had fallen deeply in love. At the time, there was no way of knowing how deep. I mean, it felt immense like a huge boulder that sits on your chest and makes it hard for you to breathe, eat, sleep—hell, makes it almost impossible to do anything. But at 16, it seems like so many things feel critical; like at any moment, one of the little flash points in your life could spark into a full-blown inferno.

When we graduated high school, we went to different colleges across the country. We toughed it through our freshman year, sending enough love letters to have decimated an entire rain forest and racking up phone bills so high AT&T should have put us on its board of directors. We saw each other on holidays and even though the magic never diminished an iota, I knew I couldn't endure another year of the agony of separation.

The week after summer vacation began, I did the single most courageous thing I'd done in my life up to that point. Juwan and I walked along the path of the arboretum near his house like we'd done so many times in the past. The sky was thick and dirty like piles of oily rags and the cicadas were buzzing continuously in the tree tops. The first time I tried to say it, the words lodged in my throat and it took another 15 minutes before I could even steady my breathing. Finally, I opened my mouth and everything came gushing out. I had forced myself to memorize a script because I had known that if left to improvise, I never would have been able to go through with this.

16

With each sentence, I felt like I was committing suicide. My words and my feelings felt like they were on escalators moving in the opposite directions. And by the time I was finished, they were so far apart, they couldn't even see each other. Standing there, holding Juwan's hand as the first raindrop found my shoulder and trickled down the back of my arm, my heart felt like it was encased in ice. He reached into my eyes with his and I could feel the pain spilling over from inside.

It thundered.

"Is there someone else?"

Of course there wasn't. There never had been from the day we kissed for the first time in this same arboretum. "Yes," I heard myself say. "It's for the best."

Unable to look at him, I pulled away from his grip and ran as the skies burst open. That was the last time I saw him.

For the rest of that summer, I was miserable. I thought that by breaking up with him early in the summer, we would have time to heal before school began again. But it took everything in me to register for classes that fall. Even then, I did miserably. By winter semester, I was on academic probation and showing no signs of improving.

"It was just puppy love, Janet," I told myself, saying it so much that I think I actually began to believe it. I finally rebounded, but I couldn't allow myself to look at any of Juwan's pictures or even think his name. Any little thing connected to him sent me into a depression. Still I fought it. I denied myself and stayed away. I told myself it was for the best. And even when I knew in my heart that that was a lie, I got good at being disciplined enough to just obey.

It took me over 10 years to realize how rare what Juwan and I had shared was. It took me 10 years to stop lying to myself and acknowledge that 'it' wasn't going away. It took me 10 years to realize that at 16 you can know love, even before you're equipped to deal with its complexities. It took me 10 years to realize that I broke up with my soul mate and that now, I needed to do something about that.

Through a friend of a friend, I found out what city Juwan lived in so there I was. I had no idea where he lived, where he worked, what he looked like. For all I knew, his hairline could have receded, his waistline could have expanded and he could be hobbling on a crutch, but it didn't matter. I was in the same city as my love and I knew that no matter what he looked like, my heart was ready to leap at the love we once shared.

For the next two weeks, I searched for a job. I had been a youth crisis counselor for two years and had done such an extraordinary job that I'd received a ream of recommendations from my former employer. While I job hunted, I hired a local private eye to find

Juwan. Exactly two weeks to the day of my arrival I received good news on both fronts; I'd gotten the job I'd applied for at an inner city community center and the investigator had found Juwan.

"Here he is," James, the private investigator, said, arranging a quartet of black and white photos on my coffee table, "Juwan Harper." In the first picture, Juwan was coming out of the front door of a house, gazing pensively over a well-manicured lawn. The photo was sharp and every detail of his face found a foothold in my memory. He looked just the way I'd remembered him—more mature, thicker in a manly way, but essentially the same. My heart throbbed longingly.

In the second picture, he was obviously stretching, his clasped hands reaching far above his head. In the third, he was turning toward the still open front door, his face almost a perfect profile. And when I looked at the final picture, my throat suddenly felt too narrow to swallow air.

"And that, Miss Smith," James said, tapping his index finger against the picture just outside the door, "is Mrs. Harper."

The tears came in a rush before I even knew they were on the way.

I wept for most of the night. How could I have been so stupid? I had to have known that a man as wonderful as Juwan wouldn't be sitting on his butt waiting for his high school lover to come traipsing back into his life. Part of me had to have realized that some woman—smarter than I was—would have found the gem I had tossed carelessly aside and treasured it the way it deserved. Yet, I had manufactured the fantasy that Juwan would see me and his fitful feelings would come swirling up from their restless slumber and engulf him. I had dreamt that we would fall into each other's arms, our souls locking together like adjacent puzzle pieces, and in a flash it would be as though we had walked out of the arboretum together that day and never parted. And as I thought those things, I wept harder.

The following morning, I awoke with a pressure headache that felt like it was going to force my eyeballs out of their sockets. I popped a few aspirin and as soon as they started working, I set to packing. The only reason why I had come here was to find Juwan and rekindle our love. Now that that was out of the question, there was no need for me to stay.

"Did you enjoy your visit?" the cab driver asked in an Indian accent on the way to the airport. I ignored him. "I hope you were able to visit the botanical gardens."

"Can we dispense with the chitchat?" I shot.

"You have let something tarnish your karma," he smiled. "Your destiny is yours to control. You must be mindful over what you allow to happen in your life."

I rolled my eyes. The last thing I needed was a fortune cookie sermon from him today. Probably because I was so irritated, his words continued to loop between my ears. Finally, about a mile away from the airport, it struck me like a charging rhino. Quickly, I fished through my purse and found the slip of paper the private investigator had given me. "Take me to McKinley Tower!"

"You thought it was stupid to have those fantasies," I muttered to myself as I stood across the street from the 20 story office building. "Well, Janet, this is stupider. Yup. You've topped yourself this time." The intersections were choked, the clog interchanging between people and cars as rush hour began to calcify. A "Where's Waldo" landscape of faces plastered the downtown streets. Even though I had made a last minute decision to at least say hello to Juwan and see if there was as much as a flicker of the flame we once shared in his eyes, I began to feel overwhelmed. Even though I knew where he worked, singling him out in this throng would be like...

His face glowed through the crowd like angels had cast a spotlight on him. He emerged from the building, his strides long and fluid. The tails of his blazer flapped in the breeze and as he stood on the corner waiting for the traffic light to change. He surveyed the crowd. There was no way he could have known I was there, but I felt like he was looking for me.

After he crossed the street, he turned in the wrong direction, walking away from me. I scurried through the maze of people, trying desperately to catch him. But as I bumped elbows with oncoming traffic and dodged the crowd surging from behind, I lost him. I wanted to cry again. I resigned myself to hailing the first taxi and going straight to the airport. Damn the cabbie and his neo-Buddhist babble! I thought. As I turned to the street, the sidewalk surged and suddenly I was stumbling backward. Someone had bumped into me, knocking me off balance. With the day I was having, my mouth was full of the brambles and as I focused my gaze to spit them, I stumbled into Juwan's eyes.

My mouth fell open like my jaw suddenly filled with lead. His cell phone was at his ear and with the other hand he was reaching to help me up. When I didn't take his hand, he scowled like he was looking at a strange animal. As if a blinding bolt of lightening had pulsed before his eyes, his vision suddenly glazed over. The smooth bronze tone of his cheeks drained to an ashen gray. His thick lips worked mutely at the receiver, before finally managing to say, "Let me call you back."

Juwan yanked me off the ground and in a single motion, locked me in his embrace. In that moment, the crowd vanished and my anxiety went fluttering off. His arms wound me tightly and I threw mine around him. I buried my head in his chest, marveling at how remarkably close this scene was to my dreams. Then abruptly, he yanked me away.

"Janet Smith!" he beamed. "I can't believe it's you!"

I smiled. "You look wonderful," I said, way too affected.

"Are you visiting? Are you here for long? When did you get here?" he fired questions at a dizzying speed.

I wanted to tell him the truth. I wanted to tell him that I had come to be with him—that I would stay forever if he would have me—that I had never stopped loving him and never would. Instead, I said, "I live here now—got a job and everything." How ditsy did that sound? But I was nervous.

"I can't believe it!" he howled. "You live in the same city as me and I didn't even know it! This is incredible." He checked his watch quickly. "Do you have time for a quick drink? I'm buying."

Of course I did.

"Barry's on the Corner" was alive with happy hour when we walked in. All the 5:01ers had staked out their places along the horseshoe shaped bar and were midway through their first martinis. We found a spot under the wide screen television. Over our first drink, we caught up on where we were. I told him about my youth counseling and he told me about his career as an equities trader.

"Any kids?" he asked.

"Nope. I'm waiting." For you!

"And you're not married," he said, pointing to my naked ring finger. "What happened? Things didn't work out with the guy you dumped me for in college?" he smiled in an attempted to show that there were no hard feelings. It didn't work.

"Juwan, I have a confession. There never was another guy. I lied to you because I thought it would be too hard for us to continue our relationship separated from each other."

His brow knuckled and his eyes cut to pondering slits as though he'd never considered the possibility. "I can't believe it. You dumped me for nothing?"

"I thought it was the best thing for both of us."

He sighed with disgust. "You did what was best for both of us without even talking it over with me? Do you know that I sat out that entire year of school after that summer? I couldn't focus on anything and every time I breathed, it felt like there were razors in my lungs."

"I know," I said, resting my hand on the back of his, "I felt the same way."

He narrowed his eyes at me. "You felt the same way? You caused both of us heartache and you say you did it for the best? Well, thanks for the help," he offered sarcastically. Juwan stood up, quickly whipped a $20 out his pocket and flipped it on the table. He turned to leave, but I took hold of his wrist.

"Don't go. Please. Let's make this better."

20

The happiness had gone from his eyes. All that was left was a cool kernel of pain; it wasn't as strong as what had been in his eyes that day at the arboretum, but you could tell it was its ancestor. "It's too late for that, Janet."

I sat for awhile feeling lonelier than I had ever felt in my life. The one reason I had had to hope had shriveled. The love of my life was gone and there was nothing that could ever fill the void that had been so wide and so deep for so long.

Outside, the traffic had ebbed. The frantic stampede had subsided, giving way to pockets of street musicians and panhandlers. I contemplated taking a cab to the airport, maxing out my credit card and buying a one-way ticket to the farthest place I could afford. And as I stood on the curb attempting to hail a taxi, I'm not sure that I had made up my mind not to do just that.

"Maybe I overreacted," the voice came from behind. "After all, that was over 10 years ago. Let me drive you home."

It was agonizing to be inside of Juwan's car—to be so close to him—and not be able to touch him. His scent radiated from his body, triggering memories that detonated like tiny explosions. Flashbacks intertwined with fantasies, giving birth to a powerful daydream that was making my collarbone moist with sweat. "I'm sorry about blowing up like that at the bar," he said, yanking me from my reverie.

I took a deep breath, collecting myself. "You had every right to react that way."

"It's just that you meant so much to me, Janet."

There was silence.

"Juwan, I didn't move here because of a job. I came here to find you. I have never gotten over you. I couldn't. For a long time, I made myself believe that what we had was puppy love and that it wouldn't have lasted anyway, but I was wrong. I love you just as deep now as I did then. No. Deeper. I had to find you. I had to know if you still dream about me. If you feel like there's a part of you that no one can touch no matter how hard they try. If you still love me."

Sitting at a traffic light, Juwan drank me into his eyes. The car suddenly felt too small for us and all of the excited energy flexing between us. The gravity of attraction drew us together and outside of our own volition, our lips met.

The feeling was like the warm blast of heat you feel when you open a running clothes dryer only this lasted longer, lingering in the scoops of my pores before being slowly absorbed. The prints of our lips matched, not like mirror images of each other, but more like the only key for the tumbler of a lock. My fingers rode down his cheek, finding the tiny prick of his early evening stubble electric.

In the middle of it all, my mind swirled through a scrapbook of memories; our first kiss sitting beneath the veil of willow branches as the sun closed out the day; the first time Juwan's lips feathered over my breasts and the way it made me want to giggle and moan on the same breath; the first time his hand rested on the inside of my thigh and how deliciously naughty I felt having him so close; the first time we made love and how it felt like I was full physically and spiritually.

You can tell so much by a kiss. Each one spins a unique tale authored by the lips of the kisser. The story being told presently was evident. The love was still there on both of our parts. It had not diminished by a fragment over the past 10 years. It was powerful and vibrant, longing to be dusted off and employed. It was fertile and strong like a seedling destined to become a mighty oak.

A horn sounded from behind. The light had changed.

Back at my place, I invited Juwan in. "I can't," he sighed.

"But the kiss... us...," I stammered.

"Janet, I'm married. I can't do this."

My smile staved off the tears. "You love her too much, huh?"

To my surprise, he shook his head. "I've never loved anyone but you. I got married because it felt like the right thing to do. My wife is a great person, but we've always been complete opposites. But we were good friends and we were both getting older so we just decided to marry. I know, it's a stupid reason to make such a commitment, but I knew that no one was ever going to fill the hole your love left in my heart. So I figured I would give her the big wedding she always wanted; make her happy."

"If you don't love her, then be with me. I'll stay out of sight. I just want any piece of you I can have."

As he smiled, a tear fell. "I can't do that. It wouldn't be fair to you or to her. If you want a piece of me, be my friend."

It felt like I was bargaining down from a Lexis to a Neon. But I agreed. I wasn't going to completely lose Juwan again.

Throughout the winter, Juwan and I kept to our agreement. We began to rebuild our friendship. We talked to each other on the phone every couple days, made a point to get together for lunch or dinner once a week and shared our highs and lows. In a lot of ways, it felt like we were dating again. My emotions wanted so badly to slough their bridal and go running freely after him, but whenever I felt too eager, I glanced at his wedding ring and let the pangs in my heart reel me back in.

When spring broke, Juwan told me that he wanted to show me a place he thought I would really like. He took me to a nature preserve and we walked the winding unpaved trails through the woods that loosely followed a stream. It wasn't quite like the arboretum back home, but with the spring flowers budding, it was like a scene from an impressionist's painting.

22

We chatted along the way before stopping at the streams source pond and sitting awhile. "Do you know how difficult it's been for me to keep my hands off you for the past few months?" he smiled.

I grinned back. "Nobody said you had to," I invited.

"Yeah, well. It was about respect. I wanted to respect Susan and I wanted you to know that I would respect you if I were married to you."

I nodded. He certainly had proven his character to me. I don't know of many men who could have been as strong as Juwan, given the circumstances. "I could never not respect you," I returned.

"That means a lot to me because there is no one whose opinion I value more. Janet, I don't know how I went 10 years without seeing your face. And being so close to you for the past few months—living in the same city and not being able to look at your pretty face everyday—has just about driven me mad." His eyes were growing misty with the depth of his sincerity.

I wanted to pull him close, hold him deep and steal him away from the world. Instead, Juwan did something that almost kicked my heart out of my chest.

"I can't take it anymore. I need to look into your beautiful eyes every day." The ring was pinched between his thumb and forefinger as he said, "Be my wife."

Noticeably absent was his wedding band.

"What about Susan?" Not the way I thought I would ever answer a marriage proposal from Juwan, but…

"We finalized our divorce Monday," he said. "We talked things out for the month after I bumped into you. Susan understood. She knew that our marriage was one of convenience. After that, it was all about hammering out the details."

I kissed Juwan deeply as he slipped the ring on my finger.

Our wedding is set for summer. In the meantime, we're doing all the things young couples in love do; finding a home, going out, laughing a lot and making a lot of love. Now, sometimes when I'm sitting at my desk in my office, I let my mind drift on how wonderful my life is.

THE END

SEX SECRET
Her Husband Is My Lover

My older sister Michelle knew that I had a crush on her husband even before they married. They started dating when I was fourteen and at the time, she thought my admiration for Derek was cute.

"One day you'll meet your own Derek," Michelle said to me, her eyes filling with tears. It was her wedding day.

Yet seven years went by and there had never been a guy that I felt could come even close to my sister's husband. I searched intently for "my" Derek, even went so far as to date a couple of men who shared the name. But none of them could ever make me forget him.

I had just returned home after graduating from college when Michelle offered to let me stay with them until I could get on my feet. Our parents had died nearly twelve years before in a car accident; since then Michelle had taken care of me as if I were her own.

I spent days job hunting and taking care of my little nephew, Mikel. He was a sweet chocolate child of three, rambunctious, full of energy and smart as a whip. In the evenings I hung out with friends or had dinner with my sister's family.

But then, the dreams started.

Derek was always there, six feet tall and powerfully built, his bronze body inviting, enticing me to do things I knew were wrong even in my fantasies.

One night Michelle, who was working towards her law degree, called the house to say she would be at the library for a few more hours than she originally planned. I was to get dinner started and watch over Mikel.

I prepared the steak and the vegetables, saving the baked potatoes for later. Derek, tall, strong and virile walked in while I was bent over the oven, marinating the steak.

"That smells good, Marie."

I tried not to smile too hard. "Michelle is going to be late tonight."

"Yeah-she's working real hard. I miss her some nights; but I know she's doing it for our future."

At eight-thirty, Michelle called to say she would be later still-could we please put Mikel to bed?

"No problem, sis." Secretly, I was happy. I wanted my sister to take her time getting home.

After Derek read him a story and I kissed him goodnight, Mikel settled in and fell asleep almost immediately. He looked like an angel with not a care in the world.

"I'm bored, Marie. Let's watch some TV." Derek winked at me outside Mikel's room.

On the loveseat, he sat comfortably nearby and flicked the remote until he found something he thought we'd both enjoy.

"So tell me why you don't have a boyfriend, Marie."

Derek said it suddenly, surprising me so much that my caramel skin flushed.

"I don't know exactly. "It" just hasn't happened yet and I'm not trying to force it."

"Good for you. Don't settle, Marie."

"I don't plan to," I said feeling bold. "Until I can get my hands on a man like my sister married, I won't ever settle down."

He laughed that low, salty bellow that always filled a room with good humor. "You don't mean that, little sis."

"I do mean it, Derek. No man I've ever met has ever been able to hold a candle to you. You're fine, accomplished and a loving family man. There aren't many brothers out there like that anymore."

His brown eyes softened as he stared at me like it was the first time. "There are more than you think, Marie. You turned into a fine woman."

"Thank you Derek."

When the kiss came, I can't be sure who initiated it exactly, but it didn't matter. What did matter were those firm, yet soft lips that hungered for mine.

He pulled me close and I melted into him, already aroused by his masculinity, his power.

He ran his hands through my hair causing flames to shoot through my body. I felt feverish; one minute I shivered, the next I burnt up and it was all for him.

"Yes, Derek. Please let it happen!"

We rolled off the small loveseat, a tan throw rug the only thing that separated our bodies from the hardwood floor.

"We shouldn't be doing this," he moaned, yet his mouth never strayed far from mine.

"This was meant to be Derek. And you know it."

His hands trailed every inch of my curvy brown body; at first, he took his time.

Yet suddenly he groaned and I felt him shiver and I knew he could no longer hold back.

With one forceful tug, my shorts and panties were around my ankles; he touched me, knowing I was ready for him.

He thrust into me, a slow, pleasantly painful pillage of my most private desires. All I could do was meet him, match him in the rhythm of our rough ride As I felt the flame growing, surrounding my entire being, he quickened his pace, his breath coming in short, tight bursts. He felt my need closing around him; Derek steeled himself, then rocked us both into a candy-coated oblivion.

"Marie, baby. We shouldn't have done that," he mumbled while still encased in my love.

"I know Derek. It can't ever happen again."

Weeks passed and Michelle was none the wiser. Derek and I managed to avoid each other; during our rare times alone together, we both felt awkward.

I felt sad at my deceit against my sister. Yet Derek was better than I had ever imagined and I was happy to have had that night with him. Despite my feelings, I remained on my best behavior.

I even went out on a couple of dates with a man I met at my new job at a marketing firm.

Jeff was sweet, smart and good-looking enough, though his lean, fair-skinned looks didn't capture my imagination the way Derek's Nubian assets did. I plodded on through pleasant conversation, dinner dates and movies with this man for a couple of weeks. He was patient but I could tell he wanted to get to know me on a more intimate level.

One night after a late movie and a bite to eat, Jeff drove to a secluded spot and stopped his Acura under a streetlight.

"Marie, we need to talk."

"About what?" I asked.

"I think you know that I like you. You're a good woman-you have it going on in so many ways. But I'm starting to get the feeling that you're not particularly that into me."

Oh Lord. How did I tell this nice man that he was right? I decided tact would be my best bet.

"You're wonderful, Jeff-you know that. We have fun together and I respect you a lot. I just prefer not to complicate things right now."

"What does that mean exactly? I don't see anything complicated about a man and a woman who like each other going to the next level."

"I wish it was that simple, Jeff."

And then something changed. He was on me, quick as a cat, grabbing and pulling, trying to kiss me. "I want you, Marie. And I'm gonna have you!"

Suddenly, I realized what this man meant to do to me. His thin frame held no hint to his massive, anger-filled strength and before I knew it, I was mashed against the passenger door, trying to wield him off.

"No! Get off of me, Jeff! You can't do this."

His hands were roaming under my red silk dress trying to creep beneath my garter. I felt him hardening with a rage-filled passion and panic flowed through me like white-hot lightning.

In my head, I heard myself asking my maker what to do-How did I stop myself from being raped?

Somehow, I found the strength to ward him off, using my small handbag to hit him in the face.

"Bitch," Jeff screamed, finally falling over into the driver's seat, his face soaked with blood.

I opened the car door and immediately lost one of my three-inch stilettos. I kicked them both off and sprinted for my life.

Three blocks away in the dark, I sat on a curb to catch my breath. And though I tried to check them, tears made their way down my reddened cheeks.

Hands shaking, I opened my bag, pulling out the device I realized probably saved me from being assaulted or worse. I used my still functioning cell phone to call my brother-in-law.

Michelle went into "mother" mode as soon as we got home-she fed me, ran a bath and attended to my every need. What I wanted most of all though was some sleep.

The next morning, I woke up to find a note on the refrigerator.

"Dropped Mikel off at a babysitter's; you need your rest. I'll be straight in from work. If you need me, don't be afraid to call. I love you, baby sis. Michelle."

The letter shook in my hands, the shame about what me and Derek had done was more alive than ever.

After talking to my employer, two uniformed police officers came by the house to take a report.

"And you're pressing charges?"

I nodded. There was no doubt.

Jeff was to be in custody as soon as they left me, if they found him. According to my employer, he hadn't shown up for work that morning.

I kept checking the doors and the windows to make sure they were locked and finally dozed off around one.

Yet, I was awake a half-hour later with a certainty that someone was in the house.

"God, Derek! What are you doing here?"

He was standing in the living room, his tie loose around his neck. On the coffee table lay videotape and sweet smelling Chinese food.

"I took a half day," I was in his arms in a second. "Thought you could use the company."

"Thank you, baby," I said, like he was my husband, like it was the most natural thing in the world.

I was not afraid of Derek and when his warm hands touched my skin. I practically melted out of my robe.

This time we went to my bedroom and locked the door.

27

I gasped for air as he took hold of me once again, his burning need bursting into me like a wave. All I could do was hold on tight for fear that I would be shaken and stirred to my very core.

And at the same time, we both released the pent-up emotion of our bond, grinding through our forbidden ecstasy, holding on to each other and the bed like writhing beasts.

After we came back to earth, paranoia immediately set in, thoughts of a surprise entrance from my sister played havoc with my pumped up imagination.

"Michelle never leaves early," Derek assured me. "You know that by now. The fact that she's attempting to make it home on time for once is simply a testament of her love for you."

For several hours we mated and cuddled, going about our afternoon as if we were a married couple.

By the time my sister walked in, there was no evidence of my dalliance with her husband. I allowed her to mother me, watching her anxiety over my well being. My shame knew no boundaries.

"Everything's going to be okay, Marie. The cops will take care of Jeff and we'll take care of you."

Michelle was right. Over several weeks I was in and out of the courts, going through the red tape that often takes place in these types of cases. Of course, Jeff denied he ever attempted to hurt me and even threatened to sue me for assault and battery.

When he went before a judge that first time, I was terrified that the cuts and swollen bruises on Jeff would sway the judge's opinion.

Yet the judge wasn't fooled, believing my story and handing down a sentence. Jeff received a year in jail, to be suspended if he completed anger management courses and began attending Alcoholics Anonymous (his attorney's suggestion).

I was livid, Jeff was in no way a drunk and used that as an excuse get away with his crime.

Immediately I decided upon a civil suit-there's more than one way to skin a cat.

When Jeff and his lawyers realized I would not back down, they agreed to a settlement. It wasn't a lot; but I was able to use the bulk of it for some choice investments.

Throughout those trying months, my secret rendezvous' with my sister's husband continued.

The day we found out that Jeff decided to settle, Michelle actually took off from work, as did Derek. That night, I joined my family for a celebration at a fine restaurant. We were all exuberant, triumphant. Even little Mikel seemed to be aware of the victory in the air.

"Happy, Auntie Marie," he kept saying, his beautiful brown eyes gazing lovingly up at me.

"Yes, I'm happy Mikel. I feel good for the first time in quite a while."

"I'm glad," my sister reached out for my hand. "Though you remained strong, I was afraid for you. I could feel your pain and I wasn't sure how to help you through that."

"I'm still working through my issues," I admitted. "But I know that life goes on. I'm going to put this entire mess behind me."

After we got home, I found that I retreated to the background. For the first time in months, I watched my sister's family interact, the obvious love they had for each other was palpable.

Michelle, home all day for the first time in years, beamed with pride at her handsome husband and beautiful son, her soft ebony features alive with tenderness. I realized then that she was living her dream-soon she'd have her law degree and the rest would be gravy.

As much as I hated to admit it, I realized that I no longer fit in there. I immediately made plans to get my own place.

"You know you're welcome here anytime, right," my sister asked several weeks later as I prepared to leave.

A flash of my naked brother-in-law assaulted my system. I knew that I was welcome.

The night before I was to move into my own place, Derek cornered me in the kitchen. I was wearing only a long t-shirt; he sported black silk pajama bottoms. I loaded my glass with ice and pulled out some popcorn. Unable to sleep that night, I decided to watch a few movies until the moving people came.

"Ready for the move, huh?"

"Been ready, Derek. I think it's time-don't you?"

"I'm going to miss you, baby. I think about you all the time. It's your body that I fantasize about."

My hands began to shake and against my better judgment, I felt my breasts responding to the sound of his voice.

Derek stepped forward, eager to touch me. "Let's go into the cellar."

I wanted to but was stopped by thoughts of my family: the beautiful laughter of my big sister and the sweet, curious innocence of my nephew as he played with his handsome father. I realized that I wanted that sense of family one day for myself. I wouldn't get it by sleeping with other people's husbands and destroying families.

"I think we both know that it's over, Derek."

"I don't know that, Marie. I care about you."

"I feel the same. But you're married to my sister. And you have sweet Mikel to think about. You do still love them, don't you?"

"Of course," He sounded indignant.

"Then act like it! Don't you realize all the damage that we've done?"

I was pacing back and forth by then, trying desperately to keep my voice to just above a whisper.

"What we've been doing is just plain wrong. And I won't do it anymore."

Derek gave me a look that only days before would have melted my soul. But he withdrew into the doorway, nodding in understanding.

"You're right, I suppose. But it was nice, wasn't it?"

"It was the best. But you're the wrong man for me. And if you plan to be the right man for my sister, you need to start acting like it." I felt my lips trembling. "We both have a lot to make up for, Derek."

I watched him slip up the stairs, back to the confines of his bedroom and back into the safe loyal arms of my sister.

After looking in on Mikel, I went back to my own room. My bags and boxes were packed up. I was finally ready to make it on my own, ready to get my own life.

THE END

FORBIDDEN ROMANCE
Our Love Could Cost Him His Job!

"**I**'m sorry it has to be this way," Paris said, easing up behind me and cinching his sinewy arms about my waist. The plump mounds of his chest padded my back as I relaxed into his warm body and let my head lull against his shoulder.

Outside the small cabin window, the sun was a lazy magenta haze on a horizon devoid of land. Ocean tides roiled into restless inkblots where it fell between the waning rays of the sun and the diluted beams of the crescent moon. At the same time, our ship, the Caribbean Queen, rocked softly like hips in a sexy slow dance.

"No worries," I said, pressing my lips against his strong shoulder. "You didn't hide anything from me. I knew what I was getting into." Paris was the ship's purser. One of his many duties was to attend to the guests and make sure they're happy. The only restriction was that he was forbidden to engage in personal relationships with the passengers. For the past 6 nights, Paris and I had been making love into the wee hours of the morning. It was safe to say that he violated that rule.

"Still, this is the kind of sunset that deserves to be seen in the open air, where you can feel its power. Instead, you're watching it through this crappy little window."

"Paris, I don't care about the sunset. I just want to be with you."

I didn't have to turn around to know he was smiling. I could feel it. The soft glow from it was warming the side of my neck, making it feel like it needed to be kissed.

The cabin lights were off. Left over haze drifted in through the window casting shadows so fat they looked like you could weigh them. I turned to find Paris awash in darkness yet his fantastic physique still making impressions like he was embossed into the night. I reached up blindly with my lips and found his waiting.

As we kissed, the tips of his fingers rolled down the length of my neck and across my shoulders. My satin robe lifted away from my skin, then tickled my calves briefly as it plummeted to my feet. He drew me near, one of his massive hands nearly covering my entire back, until my chest pressed flat against his. At the same time, his other hand smoothed easily over my bottom before coming to rest with a sharp and thrilling squeeze.

The bed was still warm when he lay me down. I fell into the indention our bodies had worn into the tired mattress over the course

31

of the past few nights. I was suddenly electric like the springs beneath me were charged with current. But it wasn't an artificial surge I was feeling; it was the natural stimulus created by two lovers with chemistry no scientist could ever define.

I gasped when he found me and growled as he made me full. The bite of my fingernails scored the back of his neck, the shores of his spine, the hemispheres of his bottom and the plank of his arms. I sucked hard on his lip as we quickened the pace and panted breathlessly into his chest as my body twitched. I rocked my hips toward his, trying desperately to match his passion. And as Paris slumped exhausted onto his elbows, I wasn't sure if the ocean had been moving us or if we had been moving it.

Diffused light gave the cabin the texture of a dream when I opened my eyes the following morning. Paris was sleeping soundly next to me, his chest rising beneath my hand as he breathed deeply. I nuzzled his cheek, enjoying the prickly texture of his unshaved face. His lips lifted in a smile even before he opened his eyes.

"What time is it?" he asked.

"Early. Just after dawn."

He groaned. "I need to get up. I have a ton to do before we dock."

Paris rubbed his eyes. Even in the near darkness of the room, his wedding band seemed to glow. For the first time since we'd been together, I felt guilty. In the beginning, I had told myself that this would be a fling. This would be something I would do while on my vacation and would leave behind as soon as the ship returned home. That Paris would return to his wife and we would never again be anything more to each other than a memory. Yet as I watched Paris slip his boxers over his incredible behind, I could feel things shifting. My guilt wasn't born from a sense of compunction or a womanly bond from one sister to another. My guilt was the product of my lust fermenting into love. I felt guilty, not because I was sleeping with another woman's husband, but because I wanted him for my own.

I needed to cool off my molten emotions before my heart melted to goo. I was going to make him tell me that I wasn't special, that I was just another port in his sailing adventures. "You're such a lucky guy," I said, swallowing the lump in my throat.

"What do you mean?"

"I mean, you get to take cruise after cruise, seeing the most beautiful islands in the world and having romances with the hottest women."

He chuckled. "It's not all it's cracked up to be. Most of the time, I'm working. So even though I'm on the ship, I don't think of it as a cruise. It's more like an office. And a lot of the time, I'm so busy that I don't get much of an opportunity to see the islands. And as for romances," he made a hissing sound. "I'm a married man. I've never done this before. You're my first."

He had to be lying! "You've got to be kidding."

Paris sat on the bed, took my hand and kissed my fingers. "Desma, is that what you're worried about? You think you're just a Caribbean fling for me?" He shook his head.

"Paris, there had to have been others. I couldn't be the first."

"Believe it or not, Sweetie, you are."

"Then why me?"

"Because you're the most…"

A knock at the door cut his sentence at the quick. If anyone found him in my room at this hour, he would be fired. He called in a deep breath and clutched my hand. "Should I answer it?" I whispered.

He looked around the room, but there was no place for a man his size to hide. Before he could answer, a second knock came. "Answer, but whatever you do, don't open the door," he said.

I went to the door and in my sleepiest voice said, "Yes?"

"Room service, ma'am."

I looked at Paris and shrugged. "I didn't order any room service," I called back.

"Is this Margo Morgan's cabin?"

I sighed in relief. "No. You're in the wrong place."

There was a pause and I heard the shuffle of papers. "I'm sorry, ma'am," he said before turning into a fading quartet of squeaky wheels.

A low snicker sliced through the tension of the moment. I turned to find Paris shaking his head and taking a look at his watch. "I thought my goose was cooked," he said.

Paris came to the door and let his soft lips light on my forehead. "I have to go. Have fun on the island and find me when you get back, okay?"

I nodded. "Paris, why? You have a great job that you love and a wife at home. Why are you risking it all to be with me?"

"You haven't figured it out yet? Think about it." He kissed me again and before I could respond he was out the door.

That night, I found myself at the bar of a small open air club on one of the larger islands. The ship was here for the night to allow the passengers a taste of the island night life. And what a perfect night for it. The moon was halved, a cool breeze swept in off the water and stars salted the sky. The small group I was with was loud and just seemed to shout, "We're tourists looking for fun!"

Steel drum music pinged around us. I confess, I don't have a single steel drum CD in my collection, but I had enough alcohol in my system to have danced to the drip of a faucet.

The only thing missing was Paris. When we docked, the ship's employees – especially the top brass – hardly ever disembarked. Tonight was no exception. Paris told me that he had a lot of the ship's financial work to cover before tomorrow because they were expecting to buy more supplies before we left port. He'd told me that he would try to make it off the boat, however, he hadn't been very hopeful. Of course, I would have had a better time with him here, but I wasn't going to let his absence prevent me from having fun all together. With one mighty swig, I downed what was left of the green concoction in my glass, pounded my palm on the bar, let loose a howl and shimmied my hips out to the dance floor.

We started off as a group of five women, dancing in a circle, most of us barefoot. Within three songs, our little wall of foreigner privacy had been invaded by the natives. Tall, lean, sun cooked men descended upon us. I'm sure we looked like the prey they're used to stalking – American women, having too much fun with inhibitions made flimsy by cheap, strong booze. We must have looked like a barrel of fish. Still, we didn't slow down a single gear. We wound our hips and popped our behinds to the beat until our sweat dampened clothes clung to our every curve.

Finally, they played a song that I recognized – a Bob Marley cover. I smiled, throwing my hands in the air as I worked out my groove. In the midst of this, I felt a sizable palm cup my derriere. I quickly swatted it away then began dancing away from the offending grope. Again, there was a hand on my bottom, this time squeezing harder. Vexed, I turned to give the nuisance a piece of my mind. When I did, I found myself looking right into Paris' face.

Anger quickly morphed into glee. I squealed and launched myself into his arms. He peeled me off of him so quickly it was almost a shove. Given my tipsy state, I had forgotten that we weren't supposed to be socializing.

"What are you doing here? I thought you had to work."

"I rushed through so I could spend some time with you."

I grinned. "Wanna dance?" I said, seductively shimmying my shoulders at him.

"I had something more private in mind." He motioned for me to follow him. He led me off the dance floor and out of the club into the darkness of the beach.

There was a rock formation where the ocean licked the stones, sending a soft mist into the air. The wall of the rock was recessed about six feet and the perfect height for sitting. We sat there, watching moonbeams play out over the tide as Paris massaged my feet. "So how did you find this little slice of heaven?" I asked.

"If you've been to these islands as often as I have, you'd pick up a thing or two too."

I snickered. "How many other things have you picked up."

He ticked his tongue at me. "None of that kind of talk. I like words like, 'My aren't you handsome in the moonlight,' or 'My neck needs your lips on it,'" he said, mock female voice and all.

I giggled. "Oh yeah? How about this, 'Mr. Paris Greendale, you make my heart flutter and skip,'" I said, sprinkling in a southern accent for fun.

He giggled. In the distance, the steel drum band was still playing. Paris took me by the hand. "Dance with me."

He held me close, his hand pressing my lower back in. The cool spray of ocean water misted over us after it struck the rocks beneath our feet. At times, it caught the rays of the moon at just the right angle to make faint, quickly dissipating rainbows before my eyes. The whole scene felt like a dream.

Paris' hand slipped down and squeezed my behind with purpose. My belly took on the role of cushion for what his thin shorts could no longer contain. I giggled again, a little embarrassed by his attraction for me and a little giddy by what I knew was to follow. "Desma," he whispered with a raspy throat, "I love being with you."

He didn't wait for me to respond. He didn't want me to. Instead, we got comfortable on the rock, ocean water misting over us and made slow love for what felt like hours.

The ship was back out to sea by the time I woke up the following day. I hadn't felt Paris get out of bed, probably a combination of the alcohol and the powerful love making. I wanted to see him badly. It was getting to the point where I wanted to be with him all the time. I showered and dressed quickly, hoping that I might run into him on deck before we docked again for the day.

The morning sun was cooking my shoulders at the same time the ocean breeze danced up my thighs beneath the skirt of my sundress. Standing on the second level of the ship, looking out over the waves, my thoughts fluttering between the heated nights Paris and I had spent and his cryptic reply to the question I had asked him the other morning.

"It seems to go on forever, doesn't it?" a heavily accented voice said from behind me.

I turned to watch one of the ship's officers approach. He was in full uniform and wore a badge that identified him as First Mate Garrison Brusseau. I nodded, "It's beautiful."

Mr. Brusseau stood beside me, leaning against the railing. "It's interesting though because it's one giant illusion. 2 or 3 hours in any direction there is land," he said, pointing for emphasis.

"Still," I smiled politely, "it's nice to get lost in the dream."

"Yes," he replied, moving too close for my comfort, "but you must remember that it's just that. A fantasy."

35

Suddenly, I realized that we weren't talking about the view anymore. I turned to walk away, but Mr. Brusseau caught my arm. "Let me go," I said, snatching away.

"Ms. Peterson, you are aware that he's married, no?"

"I don't know what you're talking about."

He made a sound like a soda bottle being opened and rolled his eyes. "His wife is a very handsome woman," he continued, not entertaining my feigned ignorance. "I've met her. She is classy, sophisticated," then his eyes rolled over me as if to say that I was no where near her league.

"Is this just an informational chat or do you have a point?"

"The point is, Ms. Peterson, that I like Paris a lot. He is the best purser I've ever worked with. However, he has been in clear and flagrant violation of the rules of conduct for this ship. I will be forced to terminate his employment if this should continue. I was hoping that you could convince him it is in his best interest to come into accordance with the regulations."

Anger tightened the hinge of my jaw. How dare he both insult me and threaten Paris in the same thirty seconds. The biggest part of me wanted to push him over the railing and into the ocean. Instead, through tight lips, I managed to press, "I'll pass on the message."

Needless to say, I didn't have much fun on the island. While everyone else milled around the open market shopping areas or slid up behind big, fruity drinks at beach bars, I sat on an outcrop of rocks, thinking. At its most fundamental level, my decision should have been very simple. Paris' job and marriage were in jeopardy because of his relationship with me. If I went away, everything would be perfect again. And yet, as easy as it sounded, I couldn't move my heart to let go. The time we had spent together on this cruise had been magical and the last thing in the world I wanted was for it to end.

By the time I headed back to the ship, I had made a decision. As much as I yearned for the opposite, I was not going to call Paris when I got back. There were only three days left in the cruise and as painful as it was going to be, I was going to spend them without him.

That evening, I stayed in my room, looking at words on the page of a book but too distracted to actually read them. I had placed a pillow over the phone because for the longest time, it felt like it was staring at me, calling me to it and imploring me to dial Paris' number. I turned fitfully in a bed that still clung to his scent and cuddled my pillow instead of his strong body.

The knock at the door startled me. Before I could stop it, a smile dove across my lips. I knew it was him and there was nothing more that I wanted. Yet, a second later, I was able to bring myself back into focus. I had to let him be.

36

He knocked again as I decided whether or not to answer. I took a deep breath. If nothing else, he deserved to know why I was avoiding him.

I pulled the door open and almost fell headlong into his deep brown eyes. "Why didn't you call me when you got back?" he asked, beginning to step inside. I stopped him.

"Paris, I don't think you should come in."

He scowled. "What? Why?"

"I just don't think it's a good idea for us to see each other anymore."

"Well, can I at least come in to talk about it?"

I shook my head. "There's nothing really to talk about. There are three days left in this cruise. I'll try my best to stay out of your way."

"Desma, you're not in my way," he protested. "What brought this on?"

"I've just been thinking, that's all. In three days, the cruise will be over and you'll go back to your life and I'll go back to mine. What we've been doing here has just been a Disney World for the heart. It hasn't been real."

"I'm sorry to hear you say that. Because for me, this is the most real I've ever felt. Yesterday morning, you asked me why I would risk my career and my marriage for what we have. The answer is because I love you, Desma."

I gasped. "You love me?"

"I can't help it. Everything I've done in my life has felt scripted. It's felt like I've done what I was supposed to do without really knowing why. But since the first day we've been together, you have made me feel alive. You've made me feel like I can do anything and be anything. I love the way I feel when I'm with you. I love the way I feel when I think about you. I just love you!"

I'm not sure who moved first, but we met at the lips. Paris cupped my face in his hands and I lassoed his waist with my arms. We stumbled into the room, spinning our bodies in a passionate dance and thumping soundly against the wall.

Our clothes melted away quickly. Who needed them? They were useless before they even crumpled to the floor. With them gone, Paris and I had more room for our lips and tongues to explore and we took turns nibbling and kissing from neck nape to toe top, enjoying every sensual moment of it.

We worked our hearts and bodies into a frenzy before allowing ourselves release. And when we did, we exploded together, churning our bodies in ways that our muscles would scold us for later. Gasping for air and eyes tearing up from overloaded neurons, we ticked the remaining spasms of pleasure out of our hips as our sweaty bodies shimmered in the dull moonlight leaking in through the slats over the windows. Paris rested his face between my breasts then puckered to kiss the bottom slope of my left breast. I stroked his head a few times then lie still, allowing my pounding heart to recover.

"So, is there a future?" I asked, breaking the silence.

"I want there to be."

"But how? I can't be your mistress. And you'll be on your way back out to sea soon. Where does that leave us?"

Paris pressed his lips against my sternum and stroked the outside of my thigh. For some reason, the combination of the two was comforting. "Desma, I'm not sure of all the answers yet but I do know that I'm not prepared to be without you now that I've found you."

I shook my head. "I want to believe Paris, but I've been in situations before where things seemed too good to be true and ..."

"But never with me," he said, cutting me off. "If I don't have a solid plan by the time we return home in three days, then you can blow me off without a second thought. But at least give me until then, okay?"

I nodded.

Then there was a knock at the door.

Tension buzzed in my ears like the hum of cicadas. Even though sweat was still slicking the back of my neck, my body was suddenly cold and rigid. "Don't move," Paris whispered.

The second set of knocks was more demanding, thundering through the cabin and seeming to be accompanied by sparks. After the encounter I'd had earlier with First Mate Brusseau, there was no doubt in my mind that he was on the other side of my door. I could almost smell his rancid odor spilling in under the door.

"What are we going to do?" I whispered.

"They can't come into a guest's room without permission. So just sit tight."

"We know you're in there, Mr. Greendale," the sharp French accent pierced the door. "Make it easy on all involved and come out."

Paris cursed so hard that it shook the bed. There was no denying that we were caught.

I jumped up and put on my robe. With the chain on the door, I opened it a crack. Garrison Brusseau's contemptuous green eyes filled the gap, the tip of his pointy nose actually reaching inside. "Mr. Brusseau, this is harassment," I spat. "I am a single woman on this cruise alone and I would appreciate it if you would leave me be before I have to report you to the captain."

He chuckled in a way that sounded like he was impersonating a garbage disposal, rolling his eyes dismissively at me at the same time. "Mr. Greendale, won't you please accompany me back to my office so that we might leave Miss Peterson to enjoy the rest of her trip." The way he said my name made my blood boil. He said it with the same inflection that you would say whore or leper.

"I'm warning you, I will report this to the captain."

Suddenly, a folded piece of paper was jabbed through the slot in the door, poking me in the forehead. "Here's a complaint form," he growled. "Fill it out and we'll investigate."

I snatched it out of his hand, throwing it on the floor behind me in the same motion. Then I slammed the door soundly, part of me hoping to pinch off the end of his nose between the door and the jamb. Immediately, he set to pounding on the door. "Jump overboard!" I shouted.

"Mr. Greendale, you were seen going into the room so I know you're in there. And I will wait here, every second of every day until we get back to port and have the authorities pry open this door if I have to. The choice is yours."

Head bowed and hope depleted, Paris wearily dressed. "Don't go out there," I pleaded. "Let's wait him out. Call his bluff."

Paris kissed me deeply, our lips holding even as he pulled away. "It's over, Desma. I have to go."

Harsh light flooded my cabin when Paris opened the door. Mr. Brusseau's gaze was equally as abrasive as he glared at Paris' submissive posture. Behind him stood two of the ships security officers, apologetic looks on their faces. Paris looked over his shoulder at me, looking more defeated than any man in love deserved to look. I wanted to go to him. I wanted to yank him back into my loving arms and save him from whatever punishment Mr. Brusseau seemed all too eager to dole out. At the very least, I wanted to kiss his lips again and somehow give him the strength to weather what lie ahead. But before I could move, Mr. Brusseau shoved Paris out of my frame of sight, looked at me with his viper-like eyes then slammed my door. I stood for a moment in complete darkness, trembling, before the tears finally started.

The following day after we set sail again, I searched the ship for Paris, but he was nowhere to be found. There wasn't even an answer in his room when I called or knocked at his door. I wanted to know what had happened to him. Had he lost his job because of me? Had they put him on probation? And even more, I wanted to know what he meant when he said, "It's over," before walking out of my door.

I was prodding my steak with my fork when First Mate Garrison Brusseau took the seat across the table from me. My steak knife was at my wrist and I had to suppress every urge in me to keep from yanking it up and jamming it into his face with one motion.

"My, my, my," he said, his words spilling sardonically from his lips, "don't we look lonely?"

"I see you didn't take my advice and jump overboard," I shot back.

"Aren't you even curious what has become of your playmate?"

"I'd rather hear it from him."

"Well, Ms. Peterson, you won't because Mr. Greendale is no longer with us."

"What do you mean?"

"I sent him home to be with his wife," he said, making me ache with the amount of pleasure he was deriving from telling me this. "When we were docked, I gave him a plane ticket. Mr. Greendale needed some time to re-evaluate his priorities."

"I hope that gets you into heaven!" I said standing to leave.

"What?"

"That holier than thou attitude!"

I didn't surface from my room for the rest of the trip. Instead of partying, I spent the remainder of the trip grieving, eating room service meals and watching old movies. The girls I'd partied with at different stops came to collect me. The first couple times, I pretended to be sick and the last couple, I just didn't answer the door.

Sure, I had been in love before, but never so deep and intense. The connection that Paris and I shared was the kind that I had always known was out there waiting for me. It was the feeling that I knew would lead to marriage. It was the kind of emotions that could last a life time. And the fact that they happened to be wrapped up in the perfect Mr. Right package only made it more devastating to lose.

Tuesday when we docked at home, I was more than ready to leave. There was nothing left for me in the Caribbean and I think I had tear soaked the linen in my cabin to the point of ruining it for good. I wanted to get back to my home, sloth off the bad feelings the past few days had burdened me with and dive back into work to numb the pain of losing someone who had meant so much to me.

Of course, Mr. Brusseau was shaking hands and wishing smiley farewells to the passengers as we de-boarded. The thought of him touching me made my stomach juices churn. I breezed through the reception line, making a point not to look at him. "Sail with us again," I heard his despicable French accent intone as I passed and I almost turned to see if he was directing it at me so that I would have an excuse to go off on him. Instead, I took the high road, refusing to look back.

As I stepped away from the pier, I took one last look at the ship. It was huge and would have been beautiful if it had not been tainted by the heartbreak that would do nothing but mar the memory of this vacation forever. If my eyes had been torpedoes, it would have been at the bottom of the ocean.

When I turned to leave, I bumped into a solid mass of flesh. I backed up a step, apology on my lips, but before I could deliver it, I choked on my words. "I like words like 'Aren't you handsome in this sunlight?'"

I couldn't believe what I was seeing. With tears in my eyes and a sob clogging my throat, I managed to say, complete with southern accent, "Mr. Paris Greendale, you make my heart flutter and skip."

He smiled then pulled me deep into his embrace.

On the cab ride back to my place, I leaned into Paris' massive chest. It felt like I was returning home. It felt like I was exactly where I was supposed to be. "Brusseau told me what happened to you."

"Yeah? They recommended me for review. Gary is a good guy but he's totally by the book. I think his wife makes him that way."

"What does his wife have to do with it?"

"Well, he met his wife on a cruise and now she's so afraid that he might meet someone else when he's onboard that she cracks the whip on him harder than the Captain."

That spineless little weasel! I wanted to turn the taxi around, find him and choke him until he turned purple. "So what are you going to do?"

"I did what my heart told me to do. I submitted my resignation," he said.

"What! But your wife?"

"These past few days have also given me time to re-think my marriage. I talked to her. Neither of us have been happy for awhile. Over the past few days, we've been able to admit that to each other. We're simply going in different directions in our lives. She's a wonderful woman, but she's just not the one for me. So we decided to go our separate ways."

"And the ship? Your job?"

"I'm going to find something on land. I want to spend all the time I possibly can getting to know you better." He kissed me. "I'm all yours." He smiled and stroked my face. Yes he was and I was going to make sure that he would be forever.

That night, we made love like the world was coming to an end at dawn. For long stretches, we moved as one, pleasing each other and crafting declarations of love in sweat and lower back flexes. We giggled and moaned, cried and gasped, glowed and melted as night petered away and morning crept over the treetops.

When I finally fell over, exhausted and happier than I've ever been in my life, Paris peeled the clinging top sheet away from my sweaty back and pressed his thick chest next to my bare skin. I stuck to him. And as I drifted off into the deepest sleep I'd had in a long time, I was lulled and comforted by the strength of his beating heart thumping gently against my spine.

Paris' divorce was final within 3 months. It was the cleanest process I'd ever seen. I mean, I'd had speeding tickets that seemed more complex than that. His wife didn't contest a thing. We even went out to lunch after they filed the final set of papers at the court house; me and Paris, her and her new boyfriend.

Paris found a job managing a 4 star hotel. It wasn't a far cry from what he had been doing on the ship and Paris did it well. Paris did most things well, as I would come to find out more and more with each passing day.

Even though we lived together from the time we left the ship, it still came as a big surprise when he proposed to me. It was a cool autumn evening and Paris had asked me to meet him at the little French Bistro that we frequented. It was a small place, but the atmosphere was incredible and the staff was friendly.

Paris was notoriously punctual, however, I arrived before him that night. Or so I thought. The hostess grinned too brightly at me when I came through the door and without as much as a word, lead me through the dining area to a table in the center of the floor. A lone candle burned on the otherwise bare tabletop. Before I could process what was going on, the hostess gusted away.

The next thing I knew, people from the surrounding tables were coming up to me, handing me long stemmed red roses. As I collected them in confusion, a cascade of whispered messages washed over me; things like, "This is so romantic!" "You've really got a good one!" "Good luck, I know you'll be happy," and "God will bless you!"

When the wave of rose bearers settled, Paris materialized. He was looking more handsome than a man should be allowed to look, dressed in a tailored suit and a tie that set off his complexion perfectly. He came to me, smile as wide as his face could handle. I should have known what was going to happen as soon as he lowered himself to one knee, however, as his body descended, I saw two people standing behind them that I immediately recognized and suddenly I couldn't think anymore. It was as if my circuits were fried.

"Mom? Dad?" I said.

"Desma, I love you." My eyes fell upon Paris' then pass to the open box he was holding in his hand. The stone glinted in the candlelight and suddenly, it hit me like a runaway train. All I could do was gasp in response. "Since the moment I met you, I have not wanted to be away from you side for a moment. Tell me that you'll make me the happiest man alive. Tell me that you'll vow to be with me until my heart no longer beats."

Through the tears in my eyes, I could see the tears spilling from his. Behind him, my mother and father were crying to. He told me later that he flew my parents in just to ask their permission. He told me that my Dad had given him a hard time – which my Dad is prone to do just to prove that he's in control – but in the end, they had given their full blessing. He told me that he had sworn to them that he would do everything he could to make me happy. I told them later that I could not imagine being any happier than I was when I was with Paris.

"I will be with you even after your heart stops beating," I replied.

The restaurant erupted in applause as Paris slipped the ring on my finger then kissed me deeply.

Our wedding date is next spring!

THE END

LOST LOVE
I'll Always Be His Second Choice!

My best friend, Tianna, came running into the video store. The moment she saw me, she waved her arms excitedly and practically jumped up and down to get my attention. "Asha, can you take a break?" she asked anxiously. "I've got to talk to you!"

I frowned a bit, but nodded my head. "Sure," I said. "I haven't taken one yet, and it's not very busy right now. But why the big rush? Is something wrong?"

"I'll tell you in a minute," she answered. "Come on, let's go across the street and get a cup of coffee."

I was manager of the video store, and could pretty much take a break whenever I wanted. Still, I took my job and responsibilities seriously. I made sure the other two employees knew I was just running across the street for a few minutes, and they could find me there if they needed me.

When we'd ordered coffee and cinnamon rolls, Tianna faced me. "I saw Latrice today," she began bluntly. "She's back in town."

I set my cup down quickly, accidentally splashing myself with the hot liquid. "She's back?" I repeated, feeling slightly sick to my stomach. "Is it just for a visit, or do you think she's here to stay?"

Tianna shook her head. "I don't know," she answered. "Candace saw her yesterday at the grocery store. I just saw her downtown just a few minutes ago…"

"Near where Eric works," I finished for her. I closed my eyes against the pain. "Is that why she's here? Does she want him back after all this time? She said she was through with him, but maybe she's changed her mind."

"I wouldn't trust her as far as I can throw her," Tianna replied matter-of-factly. "She always collected men like shades of lipstick. And she went out with Eric for almost two years. She probably still cares about him. She might want to see him again – just to catch up on old times. It doesn't mean she wants him back."

"How does she look?" I whispered, knowing the answer, and not really wanting to hear.

"Gorgeous," she admitted grudgingly. "Look, Asha, what do you expect? It's only been five years. It's not like her hair's gone gray, or she's gained 100 pounds in that amount of time."

"Well, she could have had four or five kids by now," I said grimly. "Or be madly in love with someone else." Someone besides my husband, Eric, I added silently.

"Okay, so she's back in town," Tianna said reasonably. "It doesn't necessarily mean she's here to break up your marriage. Maybe she's just visiting her family, or taking a vacation."

"And maybe she'll just happen to 'accidentally' run into Eric," I added bitterly. I paused for a long moment, then spoke softly. "I don't think he's ever gotten over Latrice. I think, deep down, he still loves her."

"Asha, he's married to you now," Tianna said gently. "Maybe he was in love with Tianna, but she was the one who dumped him and ran off to New York! She was always selfish and cold. She left so she could have a career in modeling, and she never gave Eric a second thought. He probably hates her for leaving him the way she did."

I looked at her skeptically. ""Right," I said sadly. "That's probably how he should feel about her. But I've seen the look on his face when someone mentions her name. And, last year, I caught him looking through our high school yearbook. I know he was thinking about her."

"Okay, so what?" she demanded. "Don't you ever think about Roy and wonder what life would be like if you'd stayed with him instead of hooking up with Eric?"

I shook my head. "I really liked Roy," I replied honestly. "But I don't think I ever loved him. I mean, certainly not the way I love Eric. But Eric really loved Latrice, and I know it. He never talks about it, but I know he asked her to marry him. When she turned him down, he was pretty devastated. You don't just get over something like that. Believe me, he hasn't forgotten about her – or stopped caring."

Tianna looked surprised at that. "Well, if she turned him down, that's her loss," she said finally. "He's married to you and that was his decision."

"That just makes me his second choice," I said unhappily. "And I could live with that – as long as she was in New York. But now, she's back here, and Eric is bound to run into her. What if she's changed her mind about marrying him? What if he wants to divorce me so he can have her instead?"

Tianna laughed. "Asha, that's crazy!" she exclaimed. "First of all, he loves you. He married you and you guys have a life together! Second, you don't even know if he still has feelings for her.

"Look, I didn't tell you about Latrice coming back to make you go crazy," she continued gently. "I just thought you should know in case you run into her. But you shouldn't doubt yourself, or his feelings, this way. You're beautiful and smart and sweet. Eric loves you!"

"Maybe," I agreed. "But he loved her enough once to want to marry her. And, even if you are my best friend, you have to admit she's much prettier than I am."

"Latrice is beautiful," she said simply. "She's gorgeous and sexy.

We all know that. It's the reason she left here and went to New York. She wanted to be a model or an actress, and she couldn't do it here. Living in a small town was holding her back from her big career. Remember?"

Of course I remembered! I had known Latrice Miller since we were both in seventh grade. Even then, she had been a gigantic pain in the butt! "I'm going to play the lead in Romeo and Juliet," she told me at the auditions for the school play. "I saw your name on the list to try out for Juliet, but there's really no point in your wasting your time. I'll get the role."

I was stunned, both by how rude she was to me, and how sure she was of herself. "You don't know that," I finally said.

She laughed. "I do know that," she said coolly. "You might get the part of my maid, or some other small role, but there's no way you'll get the lead."

The worst thing was, she had been absolutely right! I hated her, but I had to admit that she worked magic on stage. Even at age 13, she looked more like 19! She was a mature, beautiful woman. Her skin was the color of milk chocolate and her eyes were huge and soulful. But it was her voice that was the most enthralling. It was sweet and lilting, and captured the heart of the audience when she spoke.

Of course, that voice, and the rest of the package, always captured the hearts of the entire male population of Easton junior high school. It was a game to her. She knew she could have any boy she wanted, and she didn't care.

The only time she was really interested in a guy was when he was already going steady with someone else. If a guy provided any kind of a challenge to her, she would flirt outrageously until he was just another conquest in her book. Then, she'd dump him, and move on. .

She earned the reputation of being a "bitch," but it didn't seem to matter to her in the least. Boys still lined up to ask her out. I suppose they all hoped they would be the one to finally make her fall in love, and stop flirting with everyone else.

In high school, it just got worse. Latrice got more beautiful every year – and more talented. By this time, she was taking dance, voice and acting lessons, and getting small parts in community theater plays.

She had also started modeling for a local agency, and came in first in one of the beauty pageants held a few towns away. She seemed to have a golden future ahead of her, and I would have had to be crazy not to be jealous of her success. Still, I was pretty happy with my own life.

But when she started dating Eric Burrows, I practically turned green with envy. Eric was easily the nicest, best-looking guy in our sophomore class, and I'd had a crush on him ever since I could remember. He was friendly to everyone, and always willing to lend a hand. Somehow, Latrice hadn't gotten around to dating him. Even better, he seemed interested in me!

We were assigned to be lab partners in chemistry. When I told that to Tianna, she squealed in delight. "This is your big chance, Asha," she said. "You tell him you're having problems with the assignment. Invite him over to study with you."

"Then what?" I teased her. "Tell him I can't live without him? Ask him to go steady with me?"

"Why not?" she replied seriously. "He's not dating anyone now. You better make your move soon, before someone else gets him."

"We're just chemistry partners," I protested. "I don't even know if he likes me."

"Everyone likes you," she replied calmly. "And you like Eric. Take a chance for once, and do something daring."

"You're right," I said suddenly. "I'll invite him over to my house tomorrow afternoon."

Of course, I sounded a lot braver, and more confident, than I really felt. I had always been fairly popular with the boys at school, but I was still shy around them. It was going to take a lot of nerve to approach Eric.

But it was Eric who suggested we study together after school. "I need to get an A in this class," he confided in me. "If my grades go below a C average, my parents told me I can't play basketball. And I'm pretty sure I'm getting a D in English."

"Maybe I could help with your English grade," I offered, a bit shyly. "That's my best subject."

His eyes lit up. "Could you really?" he asked. "That would be great. You know, I don't mind reading these books, but I never get all the meanings and symbolism and things Mrs. Bracken is always asking for. Sometimes, I don't even know what she's talking about."

"And all that stuff is my favorite part," I replied truthfully. "I always like to think about what the author was trying to say to people when he wrote it. It makes it more interesting."

"Look, I could come over after school today," he said happily. "We'll work on chemistry first, then English. That would be great."

I couldn't believe how easy that had been! Eric met me at my locker after school, and grinned. "This is awfully nice of you, Asha," he said sincerely. "Everyone knows you're the smartest girl in school."

I laughed. "I don't know about that," I replied. "I know I have to work really hard to keep my grades up. Nothing comes easily."

"No, you're really smart," he said, shaking his head. "I can tell. I've noticed that you always have the right answer in class."

I looked at him amazement. "You've noticed me?" I asked in disbelief.

He smiled. "Of course," he answered. "You're not only smart, you're pretty cute as well."

I tried to stay calm, even though my insides were doing cartwheels. Eric Burrows had noticed me! And he thought I was cute!

When we got to my house, I offered Eric some of my mom's chocolate-chip cookies and a soft drink. The next three hours were like heaven to me! We talked and studied and laughed like we had been friends forever. Of course, I felt much more than that. I was already in love with him!

When Eric left that night, I really thought we had shared something special. Secretly, I was hoping it might lead to a relationship. I fell asleep that night, thinking about Eric and whether he would ask me out on a date when I saw him again.

But my hopes were dashed to the ground the very next day. Overnight, Latrice had noticed Eric, and was waiting for him at his locker. I knew she had decided Eric was going to be her next boyfriend!

Sure enough, within a week, Latrice and Eric were a couple. I don't know how she had figured out I was interested in him, but she had, and she'd moved in quickly. Whenever she looked at me, she had this really smug, self-satisfied smirk on her face. I desperately wanted to smack that look off of her!

Eric didn't avoid me after that, but it was definitely not the same when I talked to him. He seemed embarrassed by the whole situation with Latrice, and I was deeply hurt. Of course, I did my best not to show my real feelings. In fact, I even helped him write his English paper!

When the big winter dance came up, Latrice made it known that she was going with Eric. She looked right at me when she described the red velvet dress she was going to wear.

"I think I'll wear my hair up," she said lightly, wrapping a strand around her finger. "What do you think, Asha?"

I narrowed my eyes. "You want to know what I really think, Latrice?" I asked, staring straight at her. "I think you don't care about Eric any more than the last five guys you went out with. You just want to go to the dance to show off your new dress, and the fact you've gotten some other guy to go out with you."

She wasn't in the least insulted. "At least I'm going to the dance," she answered airily. "Don't be mad at me because Eric likes me instead of you."

"I'm not mad," I said truthfully. "I feel sorry for Eric. You're just using him, like you do everyone else."

That did make her angry. "You need to grow up, Asha," she said coldly. "Life is full of opportunities – but only for the people who know how to take advantage of them. Eric is the right man for me now. It has nothing to do with love."

I didn't know what to say to that. She was probably right, and I was living like a hopeless romantic. Latrice was definitely not one to miss an opportunity that came her way, and that included the men she came across off.

When I talked to Tianna about it, she made a face. "She thinks she can get away with anything because she's pretty," she said scornfully. "Look, don't let Latrice get to you. Roy Franklin wants to go out with you. Why don't you go with him to the winter dance?"

I shook my head doubtfully. "You know, Roy's asked me out before," I answered calmly. "And I'm not really interested in him like that."

"Like what?" she demanded. "You'd rather just sit around on Saturday night wondering what Eric and Latrice are up to?"

"Oh, and it would be so much better to actually watch them up close and personal?" I asked grumpily. "Then I can really make myself miserable."

She laughed. "Maybe you could try to make Eric jealous instead," she said. "Cozy up to Roy a little at the dance. Make sure Eric sees you doing it."

I had to laugh in spite of myself. "Didn't I just accuse Latrice of using men to get what she wanted?" I asked. "Now, you want me to do the same thing to Roy?"

"Roy's a nice guy," she answered. "And he likes you. You might surprise yourself by having a good time with him. That way, everyone wins."

I wasn't sure about Tianna's logic, but the idea of going to the dance with anyone, sounded better than sitting at home alone. That afternoon, I saw Roy at the library. I sat down next to him and smiled.

"Asha," he said, looking pleased and surprised. "I haven't seen you around much lately."

I shrugged. "I've been busy with homework – same as you," I answered. "I see you've got Mr. Kaye for geography."

It took about five minutes of talking and half-flirting with Roy before he finally got around to asking me to go with him to the dance. Actually, it was kind of touching how much it seemed to mean to him when I said yes. Despite my crush on Eric, I discovered I was really looking forward to going to the dance with Roy.

Tianna was thrilled when I told her. "We'll double-date," she decided quickly. "Me and Thomas, you and Roy. And I saw a great dress for you at the mall – all gold and white lace. You'll be so gorgeous in it! Eric will be sorry he decided to go with Latrice instead of you."

The dress was way more than I should have spent, but I dipped into all my babysitting savings and splurged. I had to admit it was worth it. When I put on the dress, I felt like a fairy princess.

When Roy saw me, his eyes lit up. "You look beautiful, Asha," he said softly.

I smiled. "Thank you," I said. "You look pretty good yourself." And it was true. Roy was really very handsome; tall and muscular, with smooth mocha-colored skin. Besides that, he was very sweet and thoughtful. As soon as he walked in, he handed me a corsage of miniature roses.

"Wow!" I breathed in awe. "I love it!"

The dance was wonderful. Not only was Roy attentive to me, but I could see that Eric was checking me out pretty carefully as well. When I saw Latrice frown at me, I smiled in satisfaction. Suddenly, I felt much better about things.

After the dance, Roy suggested we go get something to eat. I thought he meant a burger and fries at the local hangout. Instead, he took me to one of the nicest restaurants in town.

"Are you sure?" I asked in surprise. "This place looks very expensive."

He grinned. "Then it's a good thing I put in extra hours at the hardware store this week," he replied. "I can afford to treat you. I want to do this."

I ordered shrimp, while Roy had a steak. While we ate, we talked about a lot of different things. Then, he looked straight at me. "I'm glad you finally went out with me, Asha," he said matter-of-factly. "And it doesn't matter why."

I was puzzled. "What do you mean it doesn't matter why?" I asked. "I went to the dance with you because I like you."

He smiled. "I know I wasn't your first choice for a date," he said. "And I saw the way you were looking at Eric tonight while we were at the dance. But it's okay. I still like being with you."

I drew a deep breath. "I'm sorry if it seemed that I was more interested in Eric than in being with you," I said truthfully. "Because I had a really good time, too. And I do like Eric, or at least I did. But I think I was staring at him only because I hate Latrice so much! She's only going out with him because I liked him first."

He laughed. "She kind of has that reputation, doesn't she?" he asked. "But, you know, she's not really a threat to you. She doesn't have what you have."

I frowned. "What does that mean?" I asked. "She's so pretty, and…"

"You're prettier," he interrupted, looking deep into my eyes. "And much nicer. Look, everyone knows that Latrice just uses people. The guys don't care because, well, she has kind of a reputation for being wild. I don't think any guy seriously believes they have a future with her."

"A future?" I asked, teasing a bit. "As in a nice house with a dog, and white picket fence around the rose bushes?"

He laughed again. "Guys think about those things, too," he replied matter-of-factly. "I mean, Latrice isn't exactly the girl you want to bring home and introduce to your family."

I shook my head. "No," I agreed. "But she is exciting."

Roy reached for my hand. "I don't want to talk about Latrice anymore," he said quietly. "Or Eric. In fact, I hope they're having a great time together. Because I'm only interested in you."

From that moment on, I started looking at Roy in a different light. I had gone out with him just to go to the dance, but I realized that I really liked him! He wasn't as good-looking as Eric, but he was still very cute. Suddenly, I didn't care so much about what Eric and Latrice were doing together either!

When Roy took me home that night, he kissed me softly on the mouth. "I want to see more of you," he said. "If that's okay with you."

I nodded. "It's okay with me," I replied. Then, I reached up to kiss him. It felt so nice! I snuggled into his arms and just enjoyed the warmth of being there.

"I didn't expect this," Roy spoke up huskily.

"What?" I asked, puzzled. "For me to kiss you back?"

"No," he replied, kissing the top of my head. "I didn't expect to start falling in love with you this soon."

My heart started pounding. "Maybe it's just the dress," I whispered. "You know, it was kind of expensive."

"Maybe it's just you," he answered. Then, he kissed me again, and it felt like my head was spinning.

"You're going to have to stop kissing me," I said finally. "I can't think straight when you do that."

"Good," he said. "That's what I wanted to hear."

After the dance, Roy and I were a couple. He called me every day, and we went out as often as we could. I enjoyed being with him. He was smart and funny and sweet. But, as much as I liked him, I knew that his feelings for me ran much deeper. He was in love with me, and told me that often.

I didn't know what to do about that. I felt guilty that I couldn't return the feelings he had for me, but I honestly liked and cared about him. We never really talked about the fact that I still had feelings for Eric, but I thought that was best.

Once, in chemistry class, Eric mentioned something to me about Roy. "You guys sure hit off fast," he remarked casually.

I looked at him sharply. "What does that mean?" I demanded. "I think you and Latrice hit it off just as quickly."

He frowned. "Yeah," he answered slowly. "It's kind of funny how all that turned out. You know, I never thought…"

Just then, the chemistry teacher started talking, and interrupted whatever Eric was going to say. I leaned over to Eric. "I'm glad you and Latrice found each other," I whispered softly. "You two look good together."

It was a complete lie, of course. I wasn't glad they had found each other, and they didn't look good together – at least not to me! Still, I didn't want him to think I was jealous of Latrice. I felt humiliated enough by everything that had happened!

"Asha, that's not what I was going to say," he replied, sounding anxious. "I wanted to tell you that…"

"Ssh, the teacher's looking at us now," I interrupted. "I don't want to get kicked out of class. We can talk later."

But there never was a "later." Sometimes, I would catch Eric looking at me like there was something he wanted to say, but it just never happened. And every time I saw him with Latrice, it made my stomach ache. I knew I still had feelings for him, but there was nothing I could do about them. She had won again!

Instead, I watched helplessly as Eric and Latrice got closer and closer. For some reason, she didn't get tired of him like the other guys she'd dated. They went to all the dances and games, and he was in the front row of all her performances. I was also pretty sure they were sleeping together, but at least she didn't talk about that part of her life. I probably would have smacked her!

"I hate her!" I said to Tianna one afternoon. "She's got the nicest guy in the whole world fawning all over her, she's unbelievably beautiful and now she's got the lead in the spring play too. She's probably going to be the prom queen, even though she's only a junior."

Tianna frowned. "I don't get it, Asha," she said, sounding puzzled. "Roy is totally, head-over-heels in love with you, and he's just as fine a guy as Eric. And the rest of that stuff doesn't matter. Look, you're twice as smart as she is. Why do you care if she's prom queen?"

"I don't know," I admitted. "It's stupid, I suppose. I know Roy is great, and I really like him a lot, but he's just not Eric."

"Oh, geez," she said in disgust. "Give Roy a chance before you decide that. Have you guys, you know..?" Her voice trailed off as she looked at me with interest.

"You know we haven't, Tianna," I replied impatiently. "I'd have told you."

She laughed. "True," she answered. "Well, why don't you? I bet once you guys actually made love, you wouldn't even think about Eric again."

"What?" I asked, with a straight face. "Is that how it works? Sex makes you lose your memory?"

"Does it ever!" she answered, rolling over on the bed and grinning at me. "Trust me on that one! Thomas can make me forget my own name with his loving."

I sighed. "Okay, maybe," I said. "I know it's weird to just sit around and daydream about Eric this way. Maybe getting physical with another guy is the way to forget about the man I can't have."

"I want all the details when you guys finally do it," Tianna replied. "That's what best friends are for."

I didn't know exactly how to tell Roy I was ready to make love. But I didn't have to worry. Somehow, Roy seemed to sense a change in me. A week later, we ended up at his house.

"My parents are out of town until tomorrow night," he said softly. "We have the place to ourselves."

"We could pop popcorn and watch scary movies," I replied, with a straight face. "I always enjoy that."

"Or," he said, pulling me close to him. "We could make love until we were both exhausted."

I started to tremble inside with excitement. "Yeah," I finally managed in a half-whisper. "We could do that instead."

His eyes widened in amazement. "Really?" he asked. "You mean…"

I kissed him. "You talk too much," I interrupted, kissing him. "You need more action."

Roy didn't hesitate. He grabbed my hand and led me to his bedroom. "Sorry," he apologized quickly. "It's kind of messy."

"I don't care," I said truthfully. "It looks fine to me."

Roy sat down on the bed. "Asha," he began hesitantly. "I've never done this before with anyone."

I looked at him in surprise. "Really?" I asked. "You're a virgin?"

He laughed. "Well, yeah," he replied. "I mean, it's not the kind of thing I'd tell you if it wasn't true. I never found anyone I cared enough about before."

I smiled. "I'm glad," I said softly. "It'll be the first time for both of us. We can learn together."

"I've been thinking about this a lot," he admitted matter-of-factly. "Well, dreaming about it, really. I want it to be good for you."

"Roy, it will be good," I assured him. "I want this as much as you do."

I was nervous about what was going to happen, but then Roy

started kissing me, and I felt my whole body beginning to relax. Soon, all I could think about was the pure, physical sensation of flesh on flesh. His hands slipped underneath my sweater and cupped my breasts, expertly massaging each nipple until they hardened. I moaned with pleasure.

"Tell me what you want me to do," Roy whispered. "Where do you want me to touch you?"

I was shy at first, but Roy made me feel very comfortable about my body. I put my hand on top of his, and slowly slid it down between my legs. "Yes, that's wonderful," I whispered urgently. "Right there and just like that."

I reached to touch him as well. He was obviously aroused and ready for lovemaking; I was excited and scared at the same time. "I…I think I'm ready," I said huskily. "But…"

"Don't worry, Asha," he said softly. "We're going to go nice and slow."

Roy gently removed my clothes, and his own, then paused to admire my body. "You're so beautiful, Asha," he said, sounding awed. "Absolutely perfect. I love you so much."

Even then, naked and about to lose my virginity to Roy, I couldn't say the words I knew he wanted to hear. I wanted him, and was very much physically attracted to him. But I simply wasn't in love with him.

Roy opened the drawer next to the bed, and pulled out a condom. "I've been waiting a long time to use this," he said. "Wishful thinking, I guess."

"Then your wishes have come true," I said, smiling at him.

Roy lowered himself on top of me. "This is it," he murmured, kissing me hard. "Are you ready?"

"I'm scared," I answered softly. "But I'm ready."

"Don't be scared," he said. "We're in this together."

"Okay," I said, closing my eyes and enjoying all the sensations his hand and mouth were creating.

When Roy thrust himself into me, there was a moment of pain, then overwhelming pleasure. I felt a moan deep in the back of my throat, and my fingernails raked across his back. When it was over, I clung to Roy, and felt tears well up in my eyes.

"That was really, really nice," I finally managed to say.

Roy kissed me. "I had another word in mind," he whispered huskily. "It was more like spectacular."

"Yeah," I replied. "I guess it was. I didn't know it could be that good the first time."

The next day, I told Tianna all the details of my night with Roy. She squealed with delight. "I knew it!" she said. "I bet you forgot all about Eric for at least 15 minutes."

I laughed. "Closer to an hour," I replied, raising an eyebrow wickedly. "No thoughts of Eric at all."

"Just admit I was right," she said calmly. "And I'll be happy."

"Okay, okay," I said. "You were right. In fact, Roy is pretty spectacular, in and out of bed."

After that, I didn't think so much about Eric and Latrice anymore. Of course, I still hated Latrice with a passion. I couldn't help it. Part of my hatred was jealousy, naturally, but it ran deeper than that. She was cold and cruel to people, and I couldn't understand why Eric was so smitten with her. He seemed completely blind to all her faults.

When we graduated from high school, Roy asked me to marry him. Turning him down was the hardest thing I ever had to do, but I couldn't put it off. I also realized I couldn't continue to lead him on any longer. He needed to know we didn't have a future together.

"Roy, I can't marry you," I began quietly. "I love you, but not enough to make a marriage work. What we had together was great, but…"

"Is it Eric?" he interrupted painfully. "Is that why you don't want to get married to me?"

I shook my head. "There isn't anyone else," I answered honestly. "It's just that I can't marry you."

"I love you, Asha," he said quietly. "You'll never find anyone who loves you as much as I do. I'd make you happy."

I knew I had hurt Roy badly, but there was no other way. I knew he would find someone who would really love and appreciate him. A few weeks later, he joined the Army and left town. He said goodbye to me, but it was awkward, and I felt guilty about the way I handled it for a long time.

Tianna was obviously disappointed in my decision. "I was hoping for a June wedding," she said. "You guys were so good together."

I sighed. "But I didn't love him," I replied. "Not the way you're supposed to if you're getting married."

She made a face. "I know, I know," she answered. "But now what are you going to do with the rest of your life?"

I shrugged. "I wish I could go to college," I said wistfully. "But there's no way I can afford it. I guess I'll just keep working at the video store for a while, unless something better turns up."

Three months later, Tianna found out that Latrice was leaving for New York. She could hardly wait to tell me the news.

"Latrice has told everyone she's going to be a model or an actress," she said excitedly. "I mean, she's really going to New York. She doesn't have a job. She doesn't even know where she's going to live! Can you imagine doing something like that? It's like a movie or something."

I felt butterflies in my stomach. "Is Eric going with her?" I asked, hoping my voice sounded casual.

Tianna looked at me sharply. "Oh, my God," she replied. "You can't still be in love with him after all this time!"

"Don't be silly," I snapped impatiently. "I just wondered, that's all. They've been going together forever."

"Well, not anymore," she answered. "They broke up last night, and I heard it got pretty ugly. They had a big fight in front of her house, and he stormed off. She's telling everyone that he was way too possessive and she couldn't handle it. She said he didn't care about her dreams at all."

"I hate her," I said, without thinking. "She's so selfish!"

Tianna smiled and shook her head. "Oh, no, you don't care about Eric at all anymore," she said sarcastically. "I can tell just how much you don't care by the look on your face."

She was right, of course. Eric had never even kissed me, and I was in love with him! It made no sense at all, but there it was.

I saw Eric around town a few times after Latrice left, but he only nodded or waved. He looked so terribly sad, I felt like taking him in my arms and giving him a big hug. Finally, I decided to do something really bold – at least for me. I went to the bookstore where he worked. "Hey," I said cheerfully. "How are you?"

"I thought everyone in town knew the answer to that," he replied matter-of-factly. "It's the hottest gossip. Latrice broke up with me because I'm not supportive of her acting career."

"You're better off without her," I said truthfully.

He looked at me for a long moment. "Yeah," he said slowly. "I know. She never really loved me, and she'd have left me anyway. The practical side of me knows that. But it still hurts."

I drew a deep breath. "Have dinner with me tonight," I said quickly, before I could lose my nerve. "I can be an awfully good listener. I'll even pay."

He started to shake his head, then smiled at me instead. "I'd like that," he said warmly. "I could use some cheering up, and I've missed talking to you."

I grinned happily. "Good," I said. "I'll meet you at the Burger Barn at 7."

"Wow, a really expensive dinner," he teased lightly. "Do I get french fries too?"

"Yeah," I said seriously. "Anything you want."

I probably changed outfits about 20 times to get ready for that date. I wanted to look perfect, but not like I was trying too hard. Finally, I just pulled on my favorite pair of jeans and a soft sweater. When I saw Eric walk in the door, my heart did funny flip-flops. He was so handsome!

"Hi, Asha," he greeted me. "You look beautiful."

I was surprised and pleased by the compliment. "I've missed you," I said softly.

He smiled. "I've been right here," he said.

I shook my head. "Not really," I said bluntly. "Latrice had you on a pretty short leash."

"Is that what people think?" he asked, frowning.

"It's what I think," I answered. "But that's just me. I don't think Latrice is a very nice person. I think she used you horribly."

He grinned. "And this is supposed to be cheering me up?" he asked. "Reminding me that I've done nothing but waste my time for the last two years?"

"Yes," I said lightly. "Look at the bright side. You're free now."

He leaned back, and studied my face. "So are you," he replied. "I heard Roy left town to join the Army."

I nodded. "We broke up," I said, a bit sadly. "He wanted me to marry him, and I couldn't."

"Couldn't?" Eric repeated. "Why?"

I shrugged. "I didn't love him," I said simply.

"I asked Latrice to marry me, too," he said thoughtfully. "And I'm not really sure why. I knew she'd turn me down. Maybe I just wanted to make sure it was over."

"Is it over?" I asked hopefully.

"Yes," he said. "She's out of my life for good. She made that very clear when she left for New York."

Eric and I had a nice time that night, and agreed that it would be fun to do it again. Somehow, we just kind of started hanging around together, talking and having meals together. Soon, we were dating steadily. The first time he kissed me, I knew I was in love!

"Take it slow," Tianna warned me. "He's probably still getting over Latrice. You don't want to scare him away, or get him on the rebound."

"I hate her," I announced for at least the hundredth time. "How could she hurt him like that?"

"You should be glad she did," Tianna answered. "Now you get a second chance at him."

And I was grateful. I was deeply in love with Eric, and determined to make him mine. I hoped that Latrice would stay in New York, and as far away from Eric and me as possible!

Six months after our first date, Eric and I made love. We had been to a movie, and gone back to his apartment for a drink. When he took me into his arms and kissed me, I practically melted!

"Asha, you're so incredibly beautiful," he said softly. "You're warm and lovely and sweet. I want you."

I could only nod in agreement. Eric pushed me down on the couch, and began kissing and caressing me passionately. I felt dizzy with the sheer pleasure of his touch. When, he reached to cup my breasts, I moaned deep in the back of my throat. I wanted him to keep on touching me that way forever.

Our lovemaking was hot and urgent. I hadn't made love in months, and I needed to be held and touched. When Eric thrust himself inside of me, I cried out with pure joy.

Afterwards, I lay nestled in his arms, feeling happier than I ever had in my life. "This is why I couldn't marry Roy," I said quietly. "I love you, Eric."

"Why didn't you ever tell me how you felt?" he asked. "All the time I was with Latrice, I..."

"Let's not talk about her now," I interrupted. "Look, I don't expect you to return my feelings. It's enough that we're here together."

I don't know what Eric was going to say, because I kissed him, and moved my body on top of his. We made love several more times that night, and I ended up staying the night. When we woke up, we made love again.

Two months later, Eric asked me to marry him. In the back of my mind, I knew I was his second choice, but it simply didn't matter. I was completely and totally in love with Eric Burrows. I had more than enough love for both of us.

And we had been happy. But now, Latrice was back in town, and undoubtedly wanted Eric back. Despite the fact that we had been married for almost four years, I didn't know how Eric would react to seeing her. After all, she had been his first love.

Tianna was staring at me. "Well?" she demanded. "What are you going to do about Latrice?"

"What can I do?" I asked helplessly. "Unless Eric and I leave town tonight, he's going to find out she's here. I can't fight her."

"You have nothing to worry about," Tianna said, not sounding too sure herself. "I mean, you're married to the man."

But that didn't mean much and we both knew it. People fell in love with other people all the time and got divorced. And I already knew that Eric loved Latrice!

When I got home from work, I automatically began preparing Eric's favorite dinner of spaghetti and meatballs. When he came in, I was still at the stove, stirring the sauce. He slipped his arms around me and kissed the back of my neck.

"Mm, smells good," he whispered. "What's the occasion?"

I couldn't stop myself. "Tianna told me that Latrice is back in town," I blurted out.

He looked puzzled. "And that's why you're making spaghetti and meatballs?" he asked. "Is she coming to dinner?"

"No," I replied miserably. "I...I guess I was just trying to remind you that I love you more than she does. I bet she doesn't even know what your favorite dinner is."

"Asha, you're making absolutely no sense," he said. "Why would Latrice know my favorite dinner?"

I turned around, tears spilling down my face. "I know you love her, Eric," I sobbed. "I know I was your second choice for a wife. What I'm trying to say is that I don't want to lose you."

Eric looked at me for a split second, then burst out laughing. "Asha, you were never second choice," he said finally. "I wanted to go out with you in high school, but it got all screwed up. All of a sudden, you were dating Roy, and Latrice wanted to go out with me."

"But you went out with her for two years!" I pointed out.

"About the same amount of time you dated Roy," he reminded me lightly. "Are you saying you'd take him back if he showed up?"

"That's different," I replied. "You asked her to marry you."

"I know," he said, gathering me close. "And there hasn't been a day since then that I haven't thanked my lucky stars she turned me down. What you and I have isn't a high school romance. It's real and it's deep and it's going to last forever. We have a future together with children and mortgages and puppies..."

"Children?" I interrupted, smiling. "We never talked about children before."

Eric kissed me, long and hard. "How about you turn off the spaghetti sauce for a while," he suggested huskily. "And we start working on that part right now."

I had been silly to worry about Latrice for all this time, and I was going to tell that to Tianna first thing in the morning. Right now, though, I was going to enjoy all the benefits of married life!

THE END

SULTRY SERENADE
A Blackout Led Me Into
My Best Friend's Arms

I pushed my clammy body through the blazing, thick air on my way to the '3' train. The temperature soared above 100 degrees for the third day. I was happy my department let me leave early. It was so hot at WCRB, the station with the "Coolest in R & B." The air conditioners dripped, straining to pump the sweltering office with cool air. My train pulled into the station and I jumped in quickly to escape the heat. Of course, the car had no air conditioning and I exited the train feeling worse than when I got on. I gazed up at the towering structure that held my home at Esplanade Gardens and prayed the elevators were in working order. I was not in the mood to walk up twenty-three flights.

Without delay, I lounged on my loveseat and paid homage to the inventor of the device that breathes out cool air. Once my body was at least thirty degrees cooler, I remembered I had some chicken defrosting. I fried the chicken and made some potato salad and prepared to give my boyfriend, Kenny a call. At least he had a car with air conditioner and he could drive here in comfort.

I called Kenny's job, no answer. Maybe he was dismissed early, too, I thought. I tried his house, no luck there either. Well, last but not least, the cell phone; straight to voice mail. Maybe he was in transit. I gave up. My body was so sticky from the heat; a cold shower was calling me. The food was done so I could jump in the shower. The cool water dissolved the salt and dirt covering my body, leaving me feeling revitalized.

I don't know why I still dealt with Kenny. For the past six months all he'd been good for was a string of headaches. He was always ready with some excuse why he couldn't come to see me. I even caught him in a lie one night when he cancelled a dinner date with me. My buddy, Rondell offered to take me out that night to make me feel better. Rondell and I went to the movies and I saw Kenny with his arm around a nineteen-year old heifer, buying her popcorn. I stormed right up to him, trying to be as cool and mature about the situation, as I could. He jerked me aside, telling me the girl was his friend's little cousin from out of town and he was just doing his friend a favor. He thought I might overreact if he told me the truth. And I fell for it.

It was too hot and I was tired of trying to figure out where Kenny was. I picked up my favorite music magazine and made myself comfortable. Under the blanket of cool air, I read about some of my favorite artists, some of which I met at the radio station. I fantasized about having a number one selling CD. I've wanted to be a singer for as long as I can remember. However, I have reserved my singing for church and my shower. My aspiration to be a professional singer was my secret.

It was seven and Kenny still hadn't called. That fool better not be up to his old tricks again. I called again and he finally picked up.

"What's up?" he asked nonchalantly, as if I hadn't been calling him for the past six hours.

I wanted to wring his neck through the phone. "What's up? I've been trying to reach you all day."

"Yeah. I know."

"Well, why didn't you call me back?" Oh yeah, I was going to kill him!

"I figured if it was important you would have left a message."

"What!? How about if I just wanted to say hi?"

"Is that what you wanted to say?" he asked dryly.

He had absolutely no clue. "No. I wanted to tell you, I was home early from work and I fixed us some dinner."

"Oh. Well. I already ate," he said matter of factly.

I was losing it. Who did he think he was? "What's with the attitude, Kenny? And why didn't you answer any of my calls?"

"I was busy," he replied sharply.

"You're always busy," I stated firmly. "Listen, I don't want to argue." I softened my tone, "Why don't you bring over some Bacardi and a DVD and chill with me."

"I'm tired right now. Maybe another time."

Was that a girl I heard giggling in the background? Is someone with you?"

"Nah baby, Why are you tripping?"

"Don't baby me. I know somebody is there!" I lashed out.

"Look, I have to go. I'll talk with you later when you calm down."

He hung up. Just like that, he hung up, "How dare he hang up!"

I redialed and he didn't answer. I knew he was deliberately ignoring my calls because the third time I called, his phone was off. I was tired of his lying, cheating ass. I needed to speak to Rondell. I knew he would say, `I told you so,' but I needed to hear his voice. It always seemed to calm me down.

It's been two years since Rondell moved in next door to me. I first noticed him when I left my building on my way to the fish market. I was in the mood for some shrimps that day. Rondell was lifting a box marked "Fragile" out of a U-haul. His brown skin was glistening with sweat in the morning sun. His muscles bulged with the weight of the box. He placed the box on a dolly and his hazel eyes met mine with a gaze that sent sparks through my body. He poured water on his short locks to cool off and sent a warm smile my way, before he turned toward the truck for another box. Not bad, I thought. I continued, unsteadily on my excursion to the market. I returned quickly with my shrimps, but the moving truck was gone.

I stepped from the elevator, still cursing myself for missing the truck and ran directly into the handsome mover. I dropped my shrimps onto the mosaic tile floor. He picked up my bag and handed it to me, ever so gently. He held out his hand for me to shake and his hazel eyes seemed to twinkle.

"I'm sorry about that. I didn't see you coming. My name is Rondell. I just moved in today."

"Thank you." I watched his smile widen. I felt comfortable with him and decided to invite the "boy next door" over for some fried shrimps. Since we were both in relationships at the time, we remained close friends.

Rondell wouldn't be surprised by my call to complain about Kenny. It wouldn't be the first time. I knew exactly what his words of wisdom were going to be, but I needed to hear them again. Unfortunately, Rondell wasn't home to answer my distress call.

I worked on some song lyrics to help me get through the days disheartening events. My stomach knotted and I found it hard to concentrate. I felt pitiful. I threw on a pair of denim shorts that hugged my generous derriere just right and a blue T-shirt with Princess emblazoned in glitter on the front. I hoped that if I looked good on the outside the hurt would go away on the inside.

I headed to the corner store for a six-pack of Bacardi Silver. It was Friday night and I was about to drown myself in a pool of self-pity. The sun was nearly set and it still felt like it was one hundred degrees outside. I sauntered into the store and I could feel all eyes on me as I approached the refrigerator section in the back. The radio was playing my song "Rock the Boat" by Aaliyah. I started to hum along; singing made me feel good and I refused to let this man bring me down. I paid for my items and strutted my stuff out of the store as a treat for all of the hungry eyes that followed.

I bounced into my loveseat directly in front of the cool air. I placed the cool sweat that slid down the side of the cold bottle against my forehead. I stared at the cordless phone I held in my other hand. I had already checked for messages on both my house and cell phones, and to my disappointment there weren't any—not even a missed call.

I relaxed with my drink, as the sky consumed the sun, leaving behind an orange mist that filled the darkening sky. At the exact moment, when day became night, the entire city shut down. All that lit the city was the moon. The air-conditioner which was my salvation, no longer hummed. I made my way to my bedroom, turning light switches on along the way hoping to gain light. I fumbled in the darkness for a candle, and made my way back to my hot seat.

My cell phone rang and my heart stopped for just a second as I prayed it was Kenny. It wasn't Kenny, but I still smiled. It was Rondell.

"Hey, baby girl. You alright over there?" his velvet voiced warmed me and a smiled was glued to my face.

"I'm holding up okay," I claimed, happy to finally speak to someone

"Sorry I missed your call before. I was at the studio with some friends."

"That's okay. I just wanted to talk."

"Come over." His voice deepened as he continued, "Unless you have company."

"I'm alone," my tone filled with disappointment. "Have you eaten yet? I fixed dinner earlier."

"Same old, Tracey. Always feeding me." He laughed heartily and I joined him. "Pack it up! I'll be right there so you don't have to walk alone in the dark hall."

"I'll be waiting," I cooed before I could catch myself. Was I flirting with my best friend? Boy, this heat was getting to me already, I laughed to myself.

Rondell tapped gently on my door. I opened the door, my breath was caught in my throat and I nearly choked. The sculpted muscles of Rondell's chiseled chest glistened in the light of my candle. Of the two years I'd known him, that was the first time I'd seen him without a shirt. Damn! I screamed inside. Rondell looked sexier than the day I met him. The candle shook in my hand. He licked his lips, blew out my flame and grabbed my hand, leading me down the hall to his apartment. He pushed his door open and the room was all-aglow. A silver candelabrum adorned the top of his baby grand piano. The sweet fragrance of Jasmine scented candles hung in the air. A soft gasp escaped. Amazed, I stood still. I tingled it was so magical.

"You did all of this for me?" I uttered, surprised I found my voice.

"You sounded a little down. I thought this might cheer you up," he replied as he kissed my forehead. "Now where is that food you slaved over in this heat? I'm starved."

We sat down to eat and it wasn't long before I filled him on my phone call with Kenny.

"Tracey, you know what he's all about. You don't need me to keep telling you. You deserve better. Stop torturing yourself," he said firmly.

Unwanted tears escaped from my eyes and slid down my cheeks. Rondell walked over to me and I looked up into his eyes as he stood above me. Silently, he smoothed my runaway tears. He led me to his piano and I sat on the bench with him.

"I wrote this today. Tell me what you think."

I found myself lost in his music and the lyrics I wrote earlier flowed from my lips. "I was blinded by my own love

Could not see you for what you really were

Deaf to the lies behind your promises

You were my rock

My sunrise

My sunset

I was your fool"

The beginning of a smile as intimate as a kiss, tipped the corners of his mouth sending my pulse racing. I looked down at my hands in my lap, hoping he did not see the fiery blaze in my eyes. He lifted his long, sexy fingers from the black and white keys and covered my hands with his own. I melted under his touch.

"Your voice is beautiful," he whispered softly. He looked at me as if he was seeing me for the very first time. "You're beautiful."

His warm hands brushed the hair from my face as he lowered his head and captured my mouth with his. My lips quivered as he traced their softness with his hot tongue. His kiss sang volumes and I could not resist its passion. He released my lips leaving my mouth burning with fire. Our hot, sticky dripped with sweat. He grabbed the candelabra and kissed the back of my neck as he led me to the bathroom. He quickly removed my clothes and I stepped under the cool water he released from the shower. I watched him remove his shorts and I gasped as I gazed upon his hard body. He joined me in the shower and caressed my breasts as he kissed the hollow of my neck. His lips continued to explore my soft, caramel skin as the cool water cascaded over our hot bodies. His tongue teased my hard nipples; I shuddered needing to feel him inside of me. A serenade of ecstasy slipped from my lips as his fingers lovingly played with my womanhood like the keys of his piano.

He placed his hands under my buttocks and lifted me gently lowering my hips onto his healthy shaft. A single tear rolled from my eye as his throbbing manhood filled my trembling canal. I wrapped my legs firmly around his back and held onto the towel bar behind him. He sucked on each breast as he gently eased in and out of my sugar walls. As the passion rose I grabbed onto his thick hair and devoured his mouth sucking his tongue. I matched the rhythm of our lovemaking stroke for stroke.

With our bodies still joined, Rondell carried me out of the

bathroom and lowered our dripping bodies onto the bed.

"This is how you should be loved," he breathed passionately.

His words intoxicated me and I was drunk with joy. Fire spread to my heart. My body was flooded with uncontrollable ecstasy. I held on tighter as our bodies reached and explosive tempo. An electric shock scorched through my veins releasing a liquid fire that caused each of our bodies to quake with pleasure.

I collapsed in the arms of my best friend and lay my head against his chest. I listened as his the pace of his heart returned to normal. He caressed my hair, kissed my forehead. I smiled and the combination relaxed me and I felt my lids grow heavy. Rondell's light, peaceful snore was my signal to let sleep win.

I woke to the refreshing air blowing from Rondell's air conditioner. He entered the room looking tall and sexy with a tray of scrambled eggs and bacon that tickled my nostrils.

"Morning, baby girl. I figured it was my turn to cook you a little something."

I giggled and kissed Rondell good morning before taking a bite of the crispy bacon. "Aren't you going to eat?"

"Nah. I'm just going to lie here and bask in your radiant glow."

Rondell moved the tray after I finished my breakfast. He kissed my legs and his soft lips tickled as they brushed against my thighs. I felt my cheeks warm and I trembled; I hadn't been so happy in a long time.

"So, what do you want to do today? I vote we rent a couple of DVD's, stay in all day and make more beautiful music together," he grinned.

I closed my eyes, took a deep breath and shuddered as I recalled the events of the night before. "Sounds like fun. Let me check my messages and then I'll go home and change."

"Cool." He picked up the tray. "I'll clean up the kitchen while you're on the phone."

I had three messages. The first was from my mother wanting to know if I was okay. The next two were from Kenny. His first call was to see how I survived the blackout. The second time he called was to apologize for the way he spoke to me the night before. He wanted to take me to dinner to make it up to me. Mixed feelings surged through me. Why did I bother to check my messages?

Rondell sauntered back into the room and hopped back into the bed with me. He stopped short of kissing me. My expression must have given me away.

"What did he have to say?"

I lowered my gaze. "He called to apologize. He wants to take me to dinner?"

He gritted his teeth, "And you're thinking of meeting him?"

Confused and afraid of how Rondell would respond to my answer, I walked toward the window. "I just need to hear what he has to say."

"So call him."

Rondell didn't understand. I didn't really need to hear what he has to say. I had to see him. I had to face him and my emotions after the night I just spent in the arms of another man.

"Tracey, I'm telling you as a friend, don't go to him. He's just going to soften you up; suck you right back in. That's what guys like him do," his voice was soft and pleading.

I pulled on my shirt and shorts. "I have to go."

"What about last night, Tracey? Didn't that mean anything to you?" Pain clouded his hazel eyes.

I couldn't look into his eyes and respond to a question I didn't know the answer to. "I'll call you later."

He pulled me gently toward him and kissed me on the forehead. "Be careful, Princess."

The walk back to my apartment was a long one, although it was only two doors away. Rondell's kiss was still branded on my forehead and I wanted to turn back around. However, I knew I needed to see Kenny and make a clean break before I thought about a relationship with Rondell. I took a deep breath and picked up my phone to call Kenny. We agreed to meet at Justin's at 6:00.

I showered, tried to clear my thoughts and do some soul searching. But, the shower only served as a reminder of my night of passion. All I could think about was of my mind. I went into my room to change into something more comfortable. As soon as I walked in, a bitter jealousy stirred inside of me. I heard Rondell playing "our song" again. How could he play it for another woman? Was anything sacred to him? My phone rang and I wasn't in any mood to speak to anyone. I changed into a pair of shorts as the caller left a message.

"Tracey... I know you're there...Pick up THE PHONE... ...What was the deal leaving me in the restaurant? Who do you think you are? Tracey! If you don't pick up this phone right now, I'm not calling you again.

Don't hold your breath, Kenny. You're the least of my worries. I thought. I took the phone off the hook; I knew he would call back again. The music from Rondell's apartment stopped. I strained to hear the muffled voices. I couldn't take it anymore. I popped in "Deliver Us From Eva," and tried to enjoy LL Cool J, and his fine self. I made sure to turn the volume up full blast. But as loud as the television was, the silence from Rondell's apartment was louder. I couldn't bear it anymore, so I turned off the movie and sat in my favorite love seat and watched the activity outside my window. Even from so many

66

floors up, everyone looked so much happier than I was. Just when I thought no one cared about me, I heard my cell phone. I tripped over my ottoman trying to catch it before it stopped ringing.

"Hi baby."

It was my mother. I hoped she wouldn't pick up on my mood. "Hi, Mamma. You're up late."

"Well, I never heard from you after the blackout. I was worried. Is everything alright?"

"Yes. I just got a little wrapped up with things. I meant to call you." I was being honest.

"Wrapped up with that handsome friend of yours?" she giggled.

I sighed, "You mean Rondell?"

"What was that big sigh for? Did you two break up or have a fight?"

"Mama, we're not dating. I keep telling you that."

"Well you should be. Sometimes we let the one's right under our nose slip away. Get some rest, baby. You sound tired. I love you."

"I love you too, Mama.

I hung up. If she only knew how right she was. Humming the song, Rondell and I shared, I closed my eyes and drifted off to sleep.

A week passed without a word from Rondell. I still hadn't called him myself. I'd been working overtime at the office, so I would stop rushing home to find zero messages waiting for me. At least Kenny never bothered to call back again. I sat by the window mesmerized by the rhythm of the raindrops against the pane, matching the rapid pulse of my heart. I continued my pity party and ordered a large pie, with extra cheese, a couple of movies and curled up on my sofa under my air conditioner. I took a deep breath and thought about what my mother said. I picked up the phone and finally gave Rondell a call.

His deep voice resonated, "Hello."

My voice quivered in response. "Hi, Rondell."

"Hi, Tracey. How are you?" his tone lowered.

I could either dance around the subject or get right to the point. We'd been friends for too long to let things get this bad. I swallowed deeply before I answered. "I've been better. Can you talk?"

"What do you want to talk about?"

"I'd like to see you and talk about things. Can you come over?"

The silence from his end pulled at my heart.

I continued, desperately, "Dell, I'm sorry about last week. We can't go on like this. I can't go on like this. I know what I did was wrong and it hurt you. I can't apologize enough."

I heard a deep sigh before he finally spoke. "Do you have anything to eat?"

I bit my bottom lip and smiled. "I just had a pie with extra cheese delivered."

"Come through. I'll leave the door open for you."

I beamed, quickly changed and grabbed the pizza. I practically ran to his apartment, but slowed down just before I reached his door. I knocked before I turned the knob. Music was playing gently in the background. Rondell stood near his piano with his back to me. I cleared the dread from my throat, ready to explain.

"Tracey," he jumped in, not turning to face me. "When you left the other day, I was deeply hurt. Not only as your lover but as your friend."

"Rondell…"

He spun around, looking directly into my eyes. "Let me finish. I have listened to you complain about Kenny for years. Two years Tracey and you keep hanging in there. I couldn't tell you to leave him, because you needed to see that for yourself. Then after we shared a night together you still ran off after him."

My knees began to shake and I dropped down onto his sofa. I held my hands in my lap so he wouldn't see them shaking. "Rondell, I never meant to hurt you. You don't understand I needed to face him. I needed closure. I knew it was the only way I could move on."

Rondell sat down beside me. "Tracey, you're a beautiful woman and the best friend a man could have." He pulled my hand into his and gently kissed it before he continued. "What you don't understand is, I fell in love with you the day we first met and I looked into your green eyes. But, you loved Kenny and I had to accept that. I should have never let you leave last week to meet him. That was my mistake."

My heart raced as my dizzied senses tried to comprehend what Rondell told me. He fell in love with me. How could I have missed that? I leaned into him while I gathered my thoughts. I told him about my meeting with Kenny and how I left him with a whopping bill. Our sides burst from laughter. Rondell stopped laughing and looked into my eyes.

"I love you, Tracey Billows."

He devoured my mouth with such fiery passion, my head tingled, igniting a charge along my spine erupting into splash of white heat. I was lost in the moment until something suddenly occurred to me.

"What about the blonde I saw you with that night?"

Rondell looked at his watch and pulled me up from the sofa. "Thanks for reminding me. I almost forget. We have an appointment. It's a surprise, so don't even bother asking."

We jumped into a cab and pulled up in front of New Life Records. I had no idea what was going on so I just followed his lead. We took the elevator to the fifth floor and the blonde was standing near the reception desk, checking her watch.

"Sorry we're late, Jane. I'd like you to meet, Tracey Billows, the singer I was telling you about."

She extended her hand, "Jane Peters. Nice to meet you. Now, let's get started, we don't have much time."

I looked at Rondell, puzzled. "What's going on?" They walked me into a recording booth.

Rondell smiled and sat at the keyboard set up in the room. "Just sing like you did for me the other night. Close your eyes and let go."

It finally dawned on me what was happening. I was about to cut my first demo, all thanks to Rondell. I blew Rondell a kiss and a lone tear slid along my face. I turned toward the mike and sang my heart out.

Six months later, Rondell and I went out to dinner. Kenny was there with that nineteen-year-old girl again. She looked at least nine months pregnant. Kenny stood and a dumbfounded look filled his face when Rondell grabbed my hand, gently squeezing it giving me moral support. He sat back down without a word. The soft music playing in the background stopped and the radio deejay introduced the next song.

"You're hearing it first on WCRB. The smooth sounds of our very own, Tracey Billows along with Rondell Williams on the keyboard, with their hit debut single, "Lovin' In the Dark."

My dream came true and I had my best friend to share it with me.

THE END

SECRET PLEASURES . . .
Forever, For Always, For Love

I had been volunteering at the Porta-Meal Society for only three weeks. I felt that I had been blessed in most things, and I wanted to be able to give my time to those less fortunate. Even though I was neat and wore the very best clothes and made sure I was made up properly without being garish, I was a thick, curvy dark-skinned female that didn't fit into glamour girl mold.

I was an administrative assistant at a prestigious marketing firm that was founded by a woman, but run by men who didn't have the intellect of a brain-damaged flea. The only thing that would make them respect a dollar sign more, was if it had a set of size 38DD breasts. Most of the time, I couldn't wait to get away from all the phoniness, so volunteering gave me something do with my free time and prevented me thinking about all the nonsense that was going on at work. Another thing that made it pleasurable was Paul Santos—a medium height, burly Panamanian brother, who was older than my thirty years. I'd guessed he was around forty or so.

He had an easy manner, a bright smile, and a raucous, contagious laugh. He loved to play Scrabble. In fact, it was well known that it was how he learned English.

I'd watch him and a few other volunteers sitting at a table in the lounge area pondering over a word, or arguing about what was and what wasn't one. I didn't think he liked me, and I was sure of it when on more than one occasion, he'd left the room when I'd entered. I couldn't imagine what it could be about me that so offended him. I was an amiable enough person, and I'd intended to speak to him about it—but something always came up.

One Saturday when I walked into the volunteer food station, everyone stopped talking and looked at me. "So do I have a big bump on my nose or something?" I said, trying to be funny and alleviate the tension.

The supervisor came up to me.

"Lasondra, it's your turn to take food to Camgi Mells"

"Who?" I heard the others snicker while some turned away to keep from laughing in my face.

The supervisor put her arm around me and led me off to the side of the room. "Mr. Mells is from Africa, and he's . . . well, he's a little eccentric."

"How eccentric?" I said, squinting at her.

"He's not dangerous or anything. I guess some people just like to keep to themselves."

"So does that mean he shouldn't be on the Porta-Meal program?"

"He has diabetes and some other associated ailments, so he's on our special meals program. Paul will be driving the West Side today, so you can ride with him."

I shrugged and wondered how bad could it be? I had to assist my cousin with tending to Uncle Blue last summer when he fell and broke both of his legs. If ever there was a cantankerous, mean-natured old man, it was he. He threw food and cussed us out on a daily basis, and that was on a good day. We suffered through two long months of his abuse, but in the end, I was the one who'd managed to set him straight. Now, he calls every week just to see how I am. Mr. Mells can't possibly be as bad as Uncle Blue, I thought and hoped.

As the food packages were marked and loaded onto the small delivery van, I reviewed my checklist to make sure everything was in order, then I climbed in beside Paul. Immediately, I sensed him stiffen, and when I looked into his dark, smoky eyes, he turned and stared straight ahead.

I tried to joke as we rode, but he wasn't having any of it. Instead, he switched on the radio to a loud Latin music station.

Mr. Mells's tenement was our last stop, and it was in not the safest neighborhood. Paul got out to accompany me to the apartment, but I was pretty annoyed with his surly silence, so I declined his assistance. He just shrugged, leaned up against the delivery van, and lit up a cigarette.

My bravery—such as it was—was tested when I walked past three rough-looking men who stood so close, I could smell the faint stench of marijuana on their breath.

The elevator of course, wasn't working, and I had to climb three long flights of stairs. I found Mr. Mells' apartment, and I rang the doorbell. After several minutes when no one came, I knocked. Still nothing. I wondered if perhaps he were too ill to come to the door, and I began banging in a panicked manner and calling his name. Still nothing. I was about to go find the superintendent when I heard the inside lock being worked. The door opened a crack, and I could barely see the tall, dark-skinned figure that peered back at me.

"What do you want?"

"My name is Lasondra Franklin. I'm from the Porta-Meal program, and I've brought you your food for the week."

I was buffering myself for a confrontation, but to my surprise, the door opened, and he stood aside to let me enter. The first thing that hit me was the delightfully sweet smell in the air. The small, neat apartment was filled with the cloying scent of cloves, mint and something I didn't recognize that instantly relaxed me. I stood still for a moment, until finally, I remembered why I'd come. "May I put this away for you, sir?" I said staring up at the thin, unusually tall man.

"Yes, the cold box is there," he said with a careful command of the English language. "And no, I am not Watusi."

It was almost as though he knew what I was thinking.

"I am Masai," he announced.

I put the food away, making sure the dates were clearly visible.

I noticed the house was filled with afro centric artifacts that I was sure were from his country. The colorful gourds, the mesmerizing paintings, and even a small loom, which had a lovely beaded decoration, he appeared to have been working on.

"This is lovely, sir." I said, admiring it. A waft of fragrance hit me again, and I closed my eyes to enjoy it."

"You like my air filter?"

"It's quite relaxing."

Mr. Mells had asked me to sit down, and he offered me a glass of ginger water. "It clears the senses, and is very good for a nervous stomach," he said, handing me the glass. He told me that in Kenya, he had been an herbalist, and he was familiar with the types of flora and fauna that exacted the best fragrances or had the highest medicinal properties. I was enthralled and was listening intently, when suddenly there was a loud knock.

"Lasondra, are you in there?" It was the unmistakable accent of Paul Santos.

I had completely forgotten about him waiting for me downstairs. "It's my driver."

We both went to the door, and Mr. Mells opened it. "Are you all right?" Paul said, looking past the tall chieftain right at me.

"I fine. I'm sorry, I let the time get away."

I extended my hand to Mr. Mells. "Thank you for the ginger water and the conversation."

"You are quite welcome," he smiled, his gruff exterior softening.

Paul was already down the hall and heading downstairs. I stopped and turned to the old man. "Mr. Mells, if you don't mind my asking, why did you let me in? I was told that none of the others were ever invited in."

"You were the first to identify yourself, and you didn't say you were just going to leave the food at the door. I cannot tell how many times that has happened, and when I got there, the food had been stolen."

"I'm so sorry, sir, you should have called us. I can assure you that that will never happen again. I promise."

Paul was fuming when I got in the van. "You are very inconsiderate, this is Saturday. Might it ever occur to you that I could have something to do this evening?"

"Did it ever occur . . . ." I corrected him. "And I sincerely apologize for wasting your precious time while I assisted a poor old immigrant who has no one.

"Well, it appears he does, now." Paul spat, gunning the motor and shooting off down the street.

I requested that I be the one to bring Mr. Mells his meals, and I even decided to call on him whenever I got the chance. He seemed delighted by my visits, and soon, we became fast friends.

"The man who came to your rescue the first time you came to see me. Is he special in your life?" he asked during one visit.

"No way! He hates me, and I don't know why. I never did anything to him."

He smiled at me. "I assure you, young lady; he does not hate you. Not at all."

I explained Paul's behavior, and I even told him I didn't know why I even cared what Paul Santos thought of me. "He can just take his Scrabble game and jump in a lake for all I care!"

The old man smiled at me with patient amusement.

A few weeks later, Mr. Mells presented me with a gift.

"I made this especially for you." He said handing me a small clear bottle. "It's a special blend of acacia petals, sandalwood, and a few drops of oil of mimosa."

I sniffed the bottle, and I was well pleased. I dabbed some behind my ears and smiled. "It's delightful. What do you call it?"

"That, my dear, is for you to name."

Several days later, I was late arriving at the volunteer office, and someone else had been assigned my delivery route.

"I sent Andrice with Paul, you can help prepare the food packets," the supervisor said ushering me to the kitchen.

I had no idea why I was so irritated by the knowledge that Andrice was with Paul. Maybe it had something to do with the fact that she gushed like a Texas oil well every time he was around.

Two hours later when they returned, they were laughing together like two old friends. The hussy walked right over to me, and plopped a large packet of food on the counter. "Your old African boyfriend wouldn't even open the door for me. He said he would only take it if it were from you. It's a good thing Paul was there or I would've left it." Andrice sneered.

"I'll take it to him on my way home," I said, giving her my best killer look.

In the locker room, I changed into my jeans from the kitchen whites we had to wear when handling food, dabbed a bit of the special scent onto my neck, and went to get the food packet. As I passed by the lounge, I saw Paul leap to his feet and hurry to me. "I will drive you." It was more like an order.

"No thanks."

"I would like to drive you, it is not safe for you, alone."

After some considerable arguments back and forth, I agreed. But I told him I would find my own way home, and that he could leave after dropping me off.

I stayed with Mr. Mells for three hours. We played cards, listened to music, and he showed me how to make my own personal perfume. "Your body is your temple, it should have a personal aroma suited just for it alone," he said.

It was close to midnight when I left, and to my surprise, Paul was in his car—waiting. "I thought you were never coming out," he complained.

"Really? What did you think was going on up there?"

"I don't know!" he said with annoyance, "That old man, he is not so old that he cannot feel something for a beautiful woman."

I stared at Paul. "You . . . you think I'm beautiful?" I asked.

"Of course. All the men think so," he said, holding the car door open for me.

I tried to hold in a smile, but I couldn't. He started the car and drove down the street.

"I always thought you hated me."

Hated you? Woman, if you only knew what I feel for you, you would leave this car in an instant. Your hair, your face, your smell . . . everything about you is passion."

I laughed. "It's only my perfume. Mr. Mells made it for me. He said I should give it a name, so I call it Secret Pleasures." We drove quietly for a while when I remembered I hadn't given him my address, and I began to tell him when he interrupted me.

"I already know where you live. When you first came to the volunteer office, I followed you home."

"That can be construed as stalking," I teased. "Besides, you never talked to me, or you always left the room when I came in, and if you didn't, you just sat there glued to that damned Scrabble board."

"I didn't know what to say." He said, pulling into a space a block away from my apartment building.

"You seem to be doing okay, now." The air suddenly seemed to be charged with warmth.

"I am talking now because it is the only way I can keep from kissing you."

I looked at him. The dull light from the street lamp did something to the inside of the car, because suddenly, I wanted him to kiss me. "Maybe that's what I want." I said, huskily.

I leaned over slightly, parting my lips, and waited. Instantly, his lips were pressed tightly against mine, and his tongue was pushing past them, taking full control of my mouth. He held me as tight as the confined space allowed, and I didn't mind one bit when I felt his hand on my bare flesh. My skirt had risen high above my thighs, and he took a liberty that that I didn't resist. He breathed against my ear, telling me that he had always wanted me so much. He placed tiny kisses on my face, my neck, and my breasts. He shifted in his seat, and I climbed over him, straddling his legs as I pressed down onto his hardness.

"Chica, you will make me burst." He breathed against my neck.

Kneading my buttocks, I ground myself over him, feeling my own body lose control.

"Then come with me. Come to my apartment."

"Are you sure?"

"Are you?"

"More than anything, I am sure that I desire you above all else."

We left the car and half-ran the single block to my apartment. We were no sooner in the door when he turned me and pressed me against it, lowering himself behind me, pulling my legs apart. He pushed his face upward and began to taste me. It was too much, and I squirmed, but he held me tight, and with his tongue, he brought me to an explosive release that made me weak. There was no bed for us, not right away.

Paul tore off his clothes, and I bit back a moan of delight when I saw his earth brown, stocky firm body. His member beckoned me, and I knelt to take it. I fulfilled his need as he had mine.

I somehow managed to get my clothes off without breaking the momentum of our passion. He leaned over me, and he looked deeply into my eyes.

"I've wanted you from the first day I saw you, Lasondra. I didn't know what to say or how to act. I couldn't approach you because you showed no interest in me. Do you want me, chica? Do you?"

Words weren't enough. I lay there on my back, my breasts pointing up at him, and I opened my legs wide. Then, I reached down and opened myself even more. With a groan of what seemed like painful delight, he entered me, sliding in easily because I was still awash with my first release.

"Oh, Dios!" he said in Spanish. "You are like velvet."

I pushed up to take every bit of him inside me. I clung to him, letting my nails scrape down his back. He lunged in deeper, and when he found the bottom of the deepest part of me, he began his slow, undulating rhythm. It was almost too much to bear as his body took possession of me. With my legs wrapped around his body, I molded mine to fit every part of him. There were no spaces between us. It was like we were pieces of a puzzle that fell into perfect place!

I moved in unison with him as he nuzzled my neck.

"I love your smell. Your perfume intoxicates me."

"Secret Pleasures . . . " I breathed back at him.

"You are my pleasure, sweet one. You are like the sandy beaches of my country. The water is as pure as this passion you are giving me. At dusk and at dawn, the sky is a rainbow of soft colors that bathe you an unearthly light. I have dreamed of doing this with you in beautiful Panama," he murmured and licked my neck.

It was like that most of the night. He brought me to heights of pleasure, and then he took me down again. By the time we were in bed, I was exhausted, but he was insatiable, and wouldn't let me rest.

"Take more, chica. Take more of me, because I cannot get my fill of you," he whispered.

We tried to keep our relationship a secret, but it was as plain as the face on a factory time clock.

I was helping to prepare the food deliveries ready one day, when the supervisor came in and told me that Mr. Mells would no longer be needing our services because he had returned to Kenya. "This was sent over by the caseworker. It's for you." She handed me a small box.

I went into the locker room and opened it. Inside were several recipes for mixing my own fragrances—including the one he'd made for me. Also, there was a lovely beaded necklace that must have taken many days to complete. Last, there was a small card in neat calligraphy, thanking me for being a valuable friend, and admonishing me that I should always strive to be at peace with myself. It was signed Camji Mells.

I went to the lounge where Paul was sitting and looking over his Scrabble board. He smiled when I walked in.

"Want to play?" His eyes were dark and filled with seductive mischief.

I handed him the card, and after he read it, he rubbed my cheek gently. "You were kind to him. He will never forget that."

I will never forget him," I whispered. "After all, it was because of the scent he made for me that I got you."

Paul laughed and fiddled with the small, wooden Scrabble letters.

I took them and arranged the letters until they spelled out the African man's name: Camji Mells.

I heard a short laugh from Paul.

"What?" I asked.

"Look at this?" He shuffled and reorganized the letters.

I gasped when he was done. I looked from the board to him, then back again. I took his hand and held it tightly.

The rearranged letters of Camji Mells was Magic Smell.

And that's just what it was: a kind of magic—because it brought me a love that I had been seeking all my life!

THE END

LOVE BY
REGULATION
We were two soldiers,
punished for our love!

"Are we still on for tonight?" Staff Sergeant Curtis Bates, bent his slender five ten frame toward me and asked in a low tone, looking around to make sure no one else was listening.

"Don't stand me up again, Curtis, I mean it," I said. Curtis was my immediate supervisor; therefore we had to be careful about our relationship, because according to army regulations, our dating was in violation of that policy. Regardless, of that policy we've been seeing each other covertly for six months. In the beginning everything between us was perfect. Then about two weeks ago he began to cancel dates, or stand me up. Afterward, he would call and apologize.

"Lets meet around seven o'clock."

"Seven it is," he handed me the folder. It was only an hour until formation, so I entered the information into the computer and dropped a copy of the finished letter on the company's commander's desk. By the time I finished my tasks, Curtis was standing at my desk, hat in hand.

"Time for formation," he instructed. I shut down my computer and grabbed my hat.

"Fall in," First Sergeant commanded. Our combat boots clicked together in unison. He went to inform us that an order by Secretary of Defense states "that the service has to standardize their good order and discipline policies concerning relationships between soldiers of different ranks," he went on to say that they will fully enforce the policy.

After formation, Curtis walked up to me. "Did you hear that?" A look of concern etched across his face.

Don't worry." I assured him. We both knew that the Secretary of Defense issued the order, but there were stipulations to the regulations concerning soldiers already in a relationship, planning to get married. Although Curtis hasn't proposed, I was sure he would.

He drew a deep breath. "We definitely need to talk about this. Instead of going out, let's meet at Lamar's place," he suggested.

I nodded. Lamar Hildreth was a fellow soldier and good friend to Curtis and me. He often helped us out, escorting me to different events. It worked so well, that many people believed we were a couple.

Later that evening, I was driving along Interstate 495 arriving at Lamar's place. His spacious apartment contained a black leather sofa with matching loveseat. The mantel was covered with family photos, including one with Lamar and his five-year-old daughter, Tia, smiling cheek-to-cheek. Cream-colored walls provided the backdrop for numerous paintings. An oak finish wall unit shelved a TV, VCR, and DVD electronic system. Next to it a large green potted tree added to the ambience.

He told me to make myself at home. Curtis hadn't arrived yet. I took a seat on the sofa, making myself at home.

While I was making myself comfortable, Lamar went into the kitchen, returning with a bottle of water. He nodded at me. I shook my head no. He walked over and turned on the CD player. The sound of Luther Vandross' music flowed filled the room. As I looked at him, it always amazed me how different soldiers look in civilian clothes. Lamar was no exception. He was dressed in blue jeans and a white tee shirt that fit snugly across his broad chest. He was definitely easy on the eyes. If I wasn't involved with Curtis, I would definitely be interested in him.

Lamar and I had a wonderful time laughing and talking. Before I knew it an hour had passed, Curtis hadn't arrived or phoned. I called him on his cellular phone. He didn't answer, so I left a message on his voice mail. Where was he? I was disappointed and angry. Disappointed because he hadn't shown up; angry at myself because I was so in love with him.

One hour later, I finally heard from Curtis. He informed me that something had come up and he was unable to make it.

"Why didn't you call me back? I phoned you two hours ago."

"Regina, I just got tied up." "Tied up doing what? I thought we were going to discuss our relationship."

"We are. It's just that we cannot do it tonight."

"Curtis, something is always going on with you," I replied in the phone. "You know what just forget it" then hung up on him. Click.

I folded my cellular phone and threw it inside my purse. I was visibly upset. Lamar came over and sat beside me on the sofa, he was so close that our knees touched. There was always some attraction between us, but we valued our friendship, therefore neither of us reacted on it, therefore, I didn't object when he took me in his arms to console me.

"Why do I allow him to do this to me?" I sobbed lightly. "I can't believe him."

"Come on, Regina. Don't cry." He whispered in my ear. "You know Curtis. One of his soldiers probably got into some kind of trouble and he had to take care of it." His hand was running up and down my back to comfort me. The motion was beginning to get next to me and I managed to get out of the embrace without him noticing.

Occasionally I have vented to Lamar about my frustration with Curtis the past couple of weeks. Lamar would just listen, never offering an opinion or taking sides.

"I doubt that," I said "something else is going on."

He leaned back and looked at me. "Like what?"

"You tell me. You're his friend."

"I'm also your friend, Regina. I don't know what is going on with Curtis. All I know is, I don't like the way he has been treating you lately," He looked me directly in the eyes. Only this time, what I saw in his was tenderness and passion that I had never seen before. It made me so uncomfortable that I looked away.

Tenderly, he lifted my chin up to look at him. "You deserve to be with a man who will fill you with love and respect."

"I know Lamar," I said softly.

"Then why do you allow him to treat you the way that he does?"

"I love him" I answered honestly. I have been in love with love with Curtis since the first time I walked into the office. I flirted with him and made it clear that I was in interested in him. At first, he avoided my advances, because I work in his section, then a couple of months later, he gave in and we had our first date.

"Love doesn't hurt, Regina," his voice dropped an octave. 'If I were your man, I would always treat you like the queen that you are. When you want me, need me to be there, I would be."

My eyes stretched and a wave of heat washed over me. He leaned closer to me again. I heard his sudden intake of breath and watched his lips descend and capture mine softly. He sucked on my bottom lip and slipped his tongue into my mouth, locking with mine. I drank in the sweetness of him, angling my head, wanting more, and simultaneously he inserted his tongue deeper. I found myself purring, aching for more of his touch, and he obliged me. As wrong as it was, it felt so good, so right.

"I have dreamed of kissing you like this many nights," he said, reclaiming my lips, again, and again.

My response was to pull him toward me as I layed back on the sofa, so that he could position himself on top of me. A desire settled between my thighs as I felt his manhood. Lamar's touch was light, painfully teasing as his hands slipped underneath my shirt, and began exploring my breasts, stomach, and hips. Heat rippled through me as the flush of sexual desire coursed throughout my body. Though I thought of many reasons to make love to Lamar, I couldn't do it. I was still involved with Curtis.

My eyes popped open. I jumped from the sofa. "Lamar get up. I can't go through with this. I'm sorry." I was in a panic. What was I thinking?

Lamar was confused. He stood to his feet. "Regina, calm down. I'm sorry. I didn't mean to take advantage of the situation, but you can't deny what just happened between us. You felt something like I did."

I was up and fixing my clothing." No matter what I felt," I couldn't think straight. "I was still feeling the effects of what happened between us." I am with Curtis. I made a mistake, Lamar. Again I'm sorry."

Even as the words left my lips, I had to wonder whom I was trying to convince, Lamar or myself. Embarrassed and flustered, I quickly collected my belongings and bolted out of the door.

The next morning after formation, I avoided contact with Lamar. When I arrived in the office, Curtis was waiting for me at my desk. I didn't want to deal with him until I could figure out what was going on in my head.

"I'm sorry about last night." He spoke softly, coming up behind me. I looked at him, but didn't respond. It wasn't the time or place to discuss last night. "Step into my office."

"This isn't the time or place," I began to say, but he cut me off.

"Sergeant Nelson, step into my office." He spoke a little louder.

I cut him a hard look. I placed the folder into the basket and followed him.

Curtis went behind the desk, steadying his chair; he plopped down heavily in the black chair. The rhythm sound of a group of soldiers, marching, and singing could be heard through the open window.

"I just want to know how things are between us? I really wanted to be with you last night, but I couldn't make it. I guess I am really paranoid about this whole fraternization policy."

I didn't realize I was standing at Parade Rest while he was speaking, until he said. "Will you please stand at ease? There is no one here except you and me."

"I'm sorry Staff Sergeant," I replied with sarcasm. I was still fuming over the incident at my desk, when he pulled rank. "I was giving you the respect you so rightfully deserve."

Curtis cast me a hard glance before he spoke again. "Look, Regina," he emphasized. "I know you're upset. I can't blame you, but you're being selfish. If we're found out, you have a lot to lose."

My stomach turned over, my chest swelled; my mind raced, and shifted gears. "I know that. I'm taking just as big of a risk as you are."

He rubbed his hand across his forehead. "I'm sorry. I'm sorry. Just be patient with me."

I left Curtis office and went back to my desk. I tried to concentrate on the promotion list, but the conversation with Curtis, and the previous night with Lamar kept my mind from comprehending.

Later that afternoon, the office was a whirlwind of activity. As I worked with a soldier, I could feel someone watching me. I looked up to see Lamar standing in the doorway. I walked over to the file cabinet to pull a file, although my back was to him. I could feel his eyes piercing through me. When I turned back around the doorway was empty.

After the evening formation, I was on my way to my room upstairs in the barracks when I ran into Lamar at the bottom of the stairs.

"Regina, we need to talk."

"I said everything last night, so forget it ever happened."

"I can't do that," he cleared his throat. "I meant what I said last night, about how I feel about you. I respect your relationship with Curtis. That's why I don't think we should spend any more time together."

I opened my mouth to protest his decision but I couldn't. I understood how he came to it, but I was going to miss him, his friendship.

I nodded in agreement then said. "I understand, Lamar," I said in a soft tone. "I'm going to miss hanging out with you, talking to you."

He stepped closer to me. I swallowed the lump in my throat.

"I'm going to miss you too," he said, embracing me in his arms. The gesture caused heat to wash over me and settled between my thighs.

"What is going on?" I heard the voice behind me say, causing me and Lamar to break apart. We turned around to find Curtis staring at us with a confused look on his face.

"We were just talking," Lamar said. "That's all."

"Really?" Curtis answered, giving Lamar a look as if he didn't believe him "Nothing is going on, Curtis. You know better than that."

Curtis glanced over at Lamar then back at me.

"I will talk to you guys later," Lamar said, giving me a final glance before he left. I nodded that everything was going to be okay and walked away.

"What was that all about?" Curtis said once Lamar was out of ear shot.

"No, Curtis, the question is what is wrong with you? You know Lamar and I are friends. You had no right to treat him like that."

"I have never seen you hugging him before and just wanted to know what is going on.

"You're worried about Lamar? What you should be concerned about is our relationship," I whispered when several soldiers passed us.

"Why don't we go and talk about it?"

"Now you want to talk about it?" I sighed and rolled my eyes. "I don't think so, I have plans for the evening." I didn't really have plans, but at the moment I was angry at him, and wasn't in the mood to see or spend time with him.

Curtis frowned. "With whom? Lamar?"

I couldn't believe my ears and had heard enough. "Good bye, Curtis." I said and turned to head to my room. I had to get away from him.

"I'll call you later," he said as I walked away.

I went to my room and laid down on the bed. I had a headache. I stared at the ceiling for half an hour then fell asleep. About two hours later I woke up to the ringing of my cellular phone. I picked it up and the caller ID flashed Curtis's number. I didn't answer. I still wasn't ready to talk to him. I turned the phone off, and pulled the covers up over my head.

I walked in the office the next morning, tired. Though I had gone to bed early, it felt as though I didn't sleep at all. After Curtis phoned, I was too keyed up to sleep, and when I did finally drift back off, my dreams had been full of Lamar, and not Curtis. A warm feeling came over me when I thought of the x-rated content of at least one of the dreams. Lamar was definitely wreaking havoc on me. I woke up tangled up in my sheets.

"I called you last night. Where were you?" Curtis whispered, standing before my desk.

I didn't look up as I continued typing on the keyboard. "I went to bed early." I finally said, looking at him. "I was tired."

"I'm sorry about yesterday and the day before. I know you and Lamar are friends. I just lost it when I saw you two together."

"Was it guilt from the other night?" I said with sarcasm.

He sounded so sincere, standing in front of me, looking like a little boy caught doing mischief.

Curtis nodded. "Yes. I want to make it up to you."

I took a deep sigh and chuckled. I wasn't about to fall for another lie from him. "I don't think so, Curtis."

"I'm serious. I miss you. I want to see you. Let's meet at Charlie's?" he looked at his watch. "Nine o'clock?" He walked away not waiting for me to reply.

Hours later, I stood in the lobby of Charlie's. The club was a local hangout for military personnel. When I arrived thirty minutes early, I had it in my mind that I was going to give Curtis five minutes and five minutes only. If he didn't show, I was leaving.

Curtis strolled in the door at exactly nine o'clock. When he stopped in front of me, my heart beat kicked into a full gallop. The brother was fine with a Capital F. No matter how I tried to deny it, I was in love with him and missed him.

"Hello, Regina." He smiled, leaned down and hugged me. I couldn't stop the involuntary shiver that slid along my spine in response.

"I see you made it."

"I told you I would be here."

Curtis and I didn't stay at the club very long. We ordered a couple of drinks, talked, and danced with other soldiers in the unit. For the moment everything between us was right with the world.

The following week was the Fourth of July weekend. The post was practically empty. Curtis and I was elated at the fact that we could relax in protecting our relationship.

"Why don't we go back to your room?" he asked one night after we left the local club at 2:00 a.m.

"Curtis, you know it's against army regulations to be together in the barracks. I don't think we should take the chance." I argued. "Lets just go to your place."

Curtis response was to bend forward and brush my mouth with his. "I can't wait that long." He planted kisses on my shoulder's neck, and face. I was hesitant, swimming through a haze of feelings and desire. "I don't know, Curtis, " I managed to say as he planted another kiss on my lips. "I don't think we should risk it."

A few minutes later, as we stood beside my twin bed. I again tried to think of all the reasons why we should not be here, but when Curtis took me in his arms again, my heart beat harder, faster. I was defeated and all rational reasoning evaporated as his lips slowly descended to meet mine. Worth the risk or not, I wrapped my arms around his neck, returning his kiss.

He deepened the kiss with savage intensity, his hot, wet tongue probing deep inside my mouth. I welcomed the invasion without hesitation, sucking, matching his burning desire with my own. I was ready for Curtis. All reservation vanished and to prove it, I stepped back and stripped off my clothing, settling seductively on the bed.

In a matter of moments, he removed his clothing, joining me on the bed. "Regina, you're so beautiful. Tonight, I'm going to make love to every part of your body." His tongue flicked over one breast then the other, rousing a melting sweetness within me. Simultaneously, his hands traced a path over my skin along the lines of my waist, my hips, and then the outside of my thighs. He parted my thighs, dipping in my private treasure.

By now I was whimpering, begging for more. He removed his finger and grabbed a condom from the back pocket of his pants. Soon he entered me, gently at first. As he continued to thrust, he became more demanding and took us both on a love roller coaster ride. "Curtis," I blurted out.

Afterward, he smiled down at me and then followed it with a kiss. "Regina, that was so good."

We fell asleep in each other's arms. Luckily, I didn't listen to my inner thoughts.

The banging on the door woke us out of a deep sleep. A few moments later we were looking in the face of the Company Commander, First Sergeant, and several Platoon Sergeants.

The Company Commander stepped forward. A look of disappointment on his face. He looked at Curtis, at me, then back to Curtis.

"I want to see you both in my office at 0800 this morning. Do you understand?"

We both nodded in unison.

After they left, I confronted him. "I told you this would happen, but you would not listen to me. Now look what...."

"Will you shut up!" Curtis shouted. "I can't think with you babbling a mile a minute."

I stood rooted to the floor. Upon closer observation, I realized he was frightened. At a time like this he needed my support if we were to make it through this together. "Curtis, I'm sorry. At a time like this we have to stick together."

Curtis nodded in agreement then began to pace the small room nervously, running his hand over his head. He stopped pacing and looked at me. "Regina, you don't seem to understand my whole career just went up in smoke. My wife will probably divorce me."

My whole body went numb. I thought I was going to pass out from the news. "What did you just say?" I didn't give him a chance to answer. "Did you say your wife?" Curtis stopped pacing when he realized what he'd said. "You're married?"

He stepped toward me. I stepped back. He spread his hand out in front of him. "Let me explain."

"Let you explain? Explain what? How you conveniently forgot to tell me you had a wife." He tried to explain, but Curtis had nothing I wanted to hear. I quickly dressed and left the room.

A week later, I stood before the commander, and accepted my punishment with my head held high. Because I was an exemplary soldier, my Platoon Sergeant spoke on my behalf. As a result, my punishment was thirty days extra duty, and garnishment half my pay for several months. Curtis wasn't as lucky, because he was in a supervisor's role; he was made an example of. He lost a stripe, removed from his position, transferred to another unit, garnishment of pay for several months, and his wife filed for divorce.

A couple of months later, I ran into Lamar at the Base Exchange. I saw him around the unit, but continued to keep my distance. Today was different; he threw his arms around hugging me. I responded enthusiastically, glad to see him.

"I heard about what happened. I knew Curtis was married. I wanted to tell you, but felt I would have been out of line."

"It wasn't your place to tell me, but it was Curtis."

"Come on I'll treat you to lunch," Lamar offered.

I let Lamar lead me to the Chinese café. When they placed General Tso's Chicken in front of me," Lamar asked. "What's on your mind, Regina?"

"Curtis covered his tracks very well. I never had a clue. I mean, I knew something was wrong, but I never suspected he was married."

"You can't beat yourself up over what happened. You did nothing wrong."

"You're just being kind."

"You can't help who you fall in love with."

Lunch with Lamar was just what I needed. The more I opened up to him, the more I relaxed, and began to enjoy his company. Lamar soon became the center of my world, then a couple of months later, I received orders to transfer to Europe.

One night after passionate night of lovemaking, Lamar held me in his arms. "I received orders for Europe," he said.

I slid out of bed and went to stand by the window. "Why didn't you tell me?" I asked, staring out into the darkness. A moment later, I felt Lamar's arms around me. He turned me around into his arms to face him. "Looks like we're going to be separated."

"Ssssh," he pressed a long finger to my lips. "We're not going to be separated."

"Slight chance."

"The chances are better than you think."

"What are you saying?"

Curtis strolled over to the night stand and pulled out a black box from the top drawer. A second later he kneeled down on one knee in front of me." Regina, will you marry me?"

My breath swelled in my chest and all I could do was nod my head.

"Is that a yes?" he asked, coming to his feet.

"Yes." I nodded again.

He slid a diamond cluster on my finger and pulled me into his arms. "I love you, Regina," he said, running his fingers through my hair.

"And I love you."

Lamar and I married a couple of weeks later at the Justice of Peace. I have to thank Curtis for Lamar. If it wasn't for Curtis, I would never have met the man who is now my husband. It just goes to show that you can never judge a book by the cover, to get the whole story, you have to read the pages.

THE END

SECRET LOVERS
My Best Friend Loved Him First!

"There he is, Saundra," my best friend, Peg, giggled in my ear.

"Wow," I looked him over, my voice cracked with a sudden surge of hormones. "He really is good looking."

"Yeah, and nice, too." Her guileless face turned crimson. "Today, in the cafeteria, I accidentally knocked over my chair and he didn't tease me or make jokes about my big butt. He cavalierly picked up the seat and smiled. He told me to have a good day. He's so sweet."

"He sounds more like a teacher than one of the stupid male students here at school."

She laughed as we began the long walk between our homeroom and English. With our heads down, we self-consciously ambled passed him, allowing our lowered eyes to devour him. I couldn't help but notice Peg's observations were absolutely right. He was gorgeous! tall, broad- shouldered and sexy.

Just then as if to parody Peg's lunchroom embarrassment, a flat-footed kid brushed by her in the hallway.

"Hey watch that big butt, Peg."

Instantly, her bright smile faded and her shoulders slumped.

"Oh don't mind him, Peg." I chided, loyally. "He's a moron."

I gave her adversary a dirty look, but he was already dashing into a classroom; Peg forgotten.

"Oh, Saundra! I'm never going to find a boyfriend with this body and huge rear end. I wish I could eat any and everything and be skinny like you."

"It's just the toss of the dice, Peg. I can't help it that my DNA is full of thin genes."

"Well, I wish I had just a few of 'em of my own."

Poor Peg had such a poor self image. I don't know where or how she had gotten it, either. Like me she came from a warm, loving family. And though it was true that she was over-weight and shy, she had a killer smile and was sharp as a tack. We'd been best friends forever and now I just wanted to see her grin and be positive.

"Tell me more about the cute guy. What's his name and how did you meet him."

Immediately, she turned sunny as her words came out in a rat-a-tat staccato.

"Well, his name is Malcolm Fredericks. His parents are taking a sabbatical in the Peace Corp. Word has it that he was there over the summer, but since he's supposed to graduate this spring, he didn't want to miss any school."

"Wow!"

"Yeah, wow!" We glanced at each giddily. He was a man of the world, something we didn't see much of in our little burg. Peg continued as we came to a halt in front of my class. "Not only that, but you remember Jay-Jay Carlson, the preacher's kid? He was in our math class last year."

"Yes—a heavy set kid who bites his nails all the time?"

"I liked the way he bit his nails, made him look vulnerable, sensitive."

"Bookish, too. Just your kind of guy." I laughed, playfully bopping her on the shoulder. "Go on."

"Well Jay-Jay is his cousin and they have switched places for the semester. Jay-Jay is in Africa building houses while Malcolm is living with his Aunt and Uncle."

"What a fascinating scenario!"

"Don't you just love his name—Malcolm? Feels like a fat, thick buttery ball of chocolate, sliding around my tongue."

We broke into salacious giggles at the picture Peg had painted. Though we both loved gooey romance novels and silly boy-meets-girl movies, what the two of us combined knew about sex you could fit in a thimble. Suddenly, though, Peg stopped laughing and her melancholy mood returned.

"Oh what's the use," she shrugged, rolling her eyes in defeat. "A handsome stud like him wouldn't want anything to do with me. He's beautiful and smart, and has been all the way to Africa."

"And nice and he looks for inner beauty not, surface glitter. Besides," I repeated, turning to go into my class. "He might like big butts. You gotta go, or you'll be late for class. See you later."

"Right," she agreed sarcastically smacking her own behind. "I'll never find a date. See Ya!"

"Of course you will. You've just got to find the right guy."

She dismissed my remarks with a wave of her hand. She smiled but her posture crumpled and her head lowered, letting her long cornrows hide her face.

During the rest of the week, Peg and I kept to our usual routine. We were practically inseparable and had been since we were kids. We went to and from school together, shared a couple of classes and then spent hours at night, divulging secrets and giggling over boys on the phone. Friday night almost always found us babysitting the Peterson triplets together or sequestered into one of our bedrooms giving each other pedicures or redoing each other's hairstyle. We could talk for hours. And it didn't take long to discover that Peg had a huge, big-time crush on Malcolm.

How could anyone blame her? He was in her journalism class and took lunch at the same time she did. Unlike anyone else that Peg had ever known, Malcolm was always complimenting her intelligence and fast clever mind while completely ignoring her pudgy features and bubble butt. Furthermore, he brooked no tolerance from others who might make nasty comments about her less than svelte size. She raved about him all the time.

To my dismay, though, the more she told me about him and his sweet nature, the more I began to like him as well—despite the fact that Malcolm and I had never met. I really began to yearn for the weekends when Peg and I'd paint our toenails, dreaming up ideal dating situations that feature Malcolm as the star.

Perhaps this was childish, but true. I couldn't wait to meet him and finally got my chance during a 'don't do drugs' assembly.

"Hey Peg!" We heard a deep masculine voice as we scurried into the gymnasium. Usually, that signaled that some dimwitted student was about to sling a cruel barb toward Peg's unfortunate backside. Not this time, it was Malcolm himself. To our total amazement he was holding two vacant seats.

After a quick bewildered glance between us, we scooted in beside him.

"I was hoping to catch you," he said, smiling broadly.

"Oh, cool!" Peg was beside herself with glee and happiness. Her round face was shiny with happiness and nervous perspiration.

Although from a distance he was really easy on the eyes, up close and personal his handsome features put Denzel Washington to shame. Malcolm was really tasty, so fine. To my utter surprise he stuck out his hand to grip mine in introduction.

"Hi," he grinned with princely ease, "you must be Saundra. Peg's told me all about you. Nice that we can finally meet."

Baffled, I could scarcely think enough to mimic what he'd said to me. From his simple handshake there came an electric current that flooded my hand, then seared all the way up my arm. My vision went fuzzy and I was relieved when the principal called the room to order and the assembly began.

Not that I heard a word of what was said. I was too busy exchanging goo-goo eyes with Peg and stealing covert peeks at Malcolm. When the lights went up and the crowd stood to stretch, Malcolm looked directly at me and astonishingly wrapped his arms about me loosely.

"Hugs not drugs!"

Seconds later, he did the same to Peg. We all laughed though both Peg and I sounded like giddy fools, I'm sure.

Suddenly, feeling as bashful and tongue-tied as Peg, I simply turned to take my place in the outgoing aisle. Once more I was stunned to find strong, though hesitant fingers close over my shoulder. Turning abruptly, I nearly knocked Peg over. She glared at me, though it was without any malice.

"Um," Malcolm paused, unable to meet either Peg's or my eyes. "As Peg no doubt has told you I'm new to town. I was wondering if you ever went to the soccer games. I understand that the one this Saturday night is supposed to be a biggie. Are you going?"

Although neither Peg nor I had been to a single sporting event all year, I intuitively figured that we'd both be cheering in the stands this Saturday evening. Again, when Peg remained mute, I spoke for us both.

"Wouldn't miss it for the world! Would you, Peg?"

"No, Saundra and I go to all the games," she lied, rather badly.

Not that Malcolm seemed to notice as he added a somewhat sorrowful postscript. "Oh you two are going together."

Now no one appeared to know what to say, I just grinned as big as I could and nodded.

Still vaguely unreadable, Malcolm sighed, looking directly at me. "Would you mind if I tagged along? We could meet at the concession stand and then sit together."

Peg gasped, but still said nothing. Again I felt compelled to speak, especially when Malcolm's eyes locked onto mine.

"Sounds like a plan!" I assured him, my own heart fluttering like it was filled with mischievous puppies.

"Six o'clock?"

"Great!" I redden profusely, nudging the mute Peg.

By now the crowd had dispersed and we joined what was left of the straggling mob. With Peg hugging my right side, Malcolm eased up onto my left. "Nice meeting you, Saundra. See you in class, Peg. Got to catch my ride."

He offered an all-encompassing wink, then with one last look to me, trotted out of the gym. I went weak in the knees, my hand on fire again.

"Wow!"

"Wow, is right!"

"Do you think he was trying to ask me for a date?" Peg asked, her eyes as big as UFOs. Although I had been wondering the same thing about myself, I quickly shrugged that thought aside. After all, Peg had seen him first—even if she hadn't been able to talk or make eye contact with him.

"Maybe. He was kind of cryptic. Still, you've got to learn to look him in the eye. Speak back when he speaks to you."

"I'll try, but it's so hard!"

Oddly enough, it hadn't seemed that difficult a task when I'd been looking at him. He was cute and real dreamboat who actually seemed interested in me, too. He had proven easy to talk to and eager to listen. I felt as if I could really open up to Malcolm; talk with him as freely as I could with Peg. An unbidden image came into my mind's eye that left me imagining how it would be to kiss him, feel his strong arms around me. The vision left me dizzy.

Then, inexplicably, I was assailed by a stifling ball of guilt. Here I was fantasizing about kissing the only guy who'd ever shown an interest in Peg. What kind of a friend was I? On the way home, I wisely kept my mouth shut and pretended to listen to Peg's Malcolm-banter. Fortunately, she was so engrossed in her subject; she didn't seem to notice that I was far, far away—daydreaming about her beau.

As the soccer game approached, I tried valiantly to forget about Malcolm, not think about the way his touch had made my pulses react. But by Saturday, both Peg and I were basket cases.

"Do I look okay?" she asked me for the thousandth time. "Don't you think this blue over-shirt makes me look thinner? You know my aunt who used to be a runway model has been giving me some clothing and dieting tips. Easy for her—she's like you. She's got good genes and always looks great."

"Thanks. You look, great, too, Peg," I wasn't lying either. Her aunt had obviously given her some good advice. And I was grateful for her comments. I'd also changed outfits a dozen times before she picked me up. By the time we'd reached our designated meeting spot, I was lighted up like a Christmas tree. So was Peg.

"Hey you, two!" Malcolm suddenly jumped from behind a stadium support pole nearly scared the breath out of us—no doubt as he had intended.

"Nice blouse, Peg. Have you lost weight?"

"Why yes!" She beamed. "Three pounds. My aunt's put me on a low fat, low sugar diet."

"Cool! Keep up the good work."

"Hi Saundra," Was it my imagination or had his voice lowered, become more intimate? I couldn't tell. Still, my heart began to pound. "You look fabulous. I love your hair."

"Oh," now I was as giddy as Peg. But before I could make too big a fool of myself, I quickly turned the attention back to my friend. "Peg's my hairdresser."

His head angled toward her, yet his eyes stayed on me. "Woman of many talents. Bet you are too, Saundra."

Somehow we found ourselves being hustled along by the crowd. We quickly found some seats that had Malcolm on Peg's end and Peg next to me. We gave our attention to the field. It was so easy to get caught up in the excitement of the game—even if Peg and I didn't have a clue as to what was going on. When our colors scored we cheered as loudly as anyone; when the other team took the ball, we booed and hissed like pros. It was exhilarating.

As halftime entertainment began to line up along the sides, Peg announced she needed fuel. And though she tried to entice Malcolm to go with her to the concession stand, he declined and made my apologies as well. Selfishly, I didn't argue, but I paid a heavy fine in the guilt department. Peg looked vaguely woebegone beneath her smile. But she had painted herself into a corner and went on down alone.

A slight silence overcame Malcolm and me as we stood in the bleachers, shifting from foot to foot. Perhaps, we were both too bashful to speak. Though my mind sifted through all the magazine articles I'd ever read, advising girls like me about boys and being alone with them I couldn't think of a single thing to say. Thank goodness Malcolm did.

"Gee Saundra," he blurted out rapidly. "You have the most amazing smile. I just love the way the corners of your mouth turn up all the time. It's like you have pixie blood flowing in your veins."

Instantly, he turned red as a tomato and stared off at something way over my head. Nobody had ever paid me such a compliment and I, too, felt the heat creep up my neck and splash all over my cheeks.

"What a lovely thing to say," I admitted honestly. Then shyness overtook me and forced my chin to my chest. Despite my embarrassment, I felt Malcolm's index finger fit shakily under my chin. "But I guess I should expect that from you. Peg's always going on about what a wonderful guy you are."

"Oh." He lifted a beefy shoulder, his eyes once again on mine. "Peg's a sweetie. She kind of reminds me of my cousin, Jay-Jay. He's a great guy, fabulous personality and funny as all get out. But he, too, has a bit of a weight problem and most girls can't quite get over that to date him. It is a killer to his self-esteem. I figure it's even worse for a girl."

"Yes," I nodded. "It is."

Before I could ask more about his feelings for Peg, he started talking again.

"Speaking of Peg," he shrugged. "Like I said she's great. But I don't want to spend all of our alone time talking about her and Jay-Jay. In fact, one of the reasons I actually noticed her at all was because of you. I found out she is your best friend and I've been eyeballing you since the first day of school. I wanted to meet you and I figured she'd get me in."

I totally didn't know how to react. I was flattered beyond my wildest dreams that such a fine guy had ever even noticed me. Yet, just the thought of betraying Peg cast a heavy dark shroud over my blossoming love. So while I might be dancing on a cloud, Peg would be crying under one. What a hideous dilemma!

Nonetheless, Malcolm hardly gave me time to think about it as we both saw Peg reenter the stadium. Quickly, he touched my shoulder and nervously blurted. "I was wondering if you, you alone, would like to go to the movies with me Sunday afternoon. Maybe stop for a bite to eat afterwards?"

This was the very first time anyone had ever asked me out for a date. I was flabbergasted, overjoyed and my voice came out in a squeak. Some odd force of Nature suddenly shook all thoughts from my head except one.

"Oh, Malcolm, I'd loved to. What time will you pick me up?"

Clearly, he was relieved by my answer and instantly recited movie times and pick up calculations. We agreed on one, just as Peg spotted us and started huffing and puffing our way. The nearer she got, the more shameful I became. She was my best friend and there was no way I wanted to hurt her. Still, on the other hand, a girl only gets one first date with a fabulous guy. Though my chest constricted and my face blazed crimson, I turned to Malcolm.

"Let's not tell Peg about our date, okay?"

"Why not?"

Since I couldn't come up with a real answer, I just batted my eyes and pouted my bottom lip. "Please?"

My flirty-girly tactics found their mark. And though he remained somewhat puzzled, he shrugged his compliance.

"All right."

As the three of us were reunited, all of us noticed the subtle movement when Malcolm moved to stand between us two girls. It was a heady moment for me and I simply could not look at Peg. Nevertheless, a wave of shame washed over me. Malcolm of course lived under no such feelings. And I was greatly appreciative of him, when he accepted a large handful of popcorn while offering a lovely little compliment that assuaged Peg's dear heart.

Oddly enough as the hour of my big first date arrived, I missed Peg's support and help. I threw outfit after outfit into a heap on my floor, trying to decide what would show off my best features. Naturally, at the same time I was consumed with how I should speak with Malcolm when we were alone. I'd never been so scared in my whole life and I wished with all my heart that I had my best friend to discuss these things with. Meanwhile I was desperate to dislodging that knot of dishonor toward Peg lurking in the recesses of my brain.

By the time I was on my way to the movies with Malcolm, I had managed to pull myself together and calm the migrating butterflies churning in my stomach. For a time I even pushed Peg out of the picture. Fortunately conversation with Malcolm was not as difficult as I had assumed.

"That was a great movie, Malcolm," I observed as we meandered down Main Street to a fast food restaurant. Actually, I was nearly skipping with joy. During the flick, Malcolm had put his arm around my shoulders and pulled me close to him. He never let go. Indeed, even now we laced fingers. His close proximity had my nerves all a-jangle. It was heavenly.

"I thought when the slasher came out of the basement you got a little scared."

"Oh, how could I be very scared with you around to protect me?"

We both blushed then Malcolm squeezed my hand. As we chowed down on our burgers and fries, I asked about his life and family and how he was adjusting to his current situation.

"It's pretty nice. I do miss my parents though and even my cousin Jay-Jay." He was pensive for a moment, adding. "It's a whole different world over there. I'm glad to have had the experience, but in all honesty, I was very glad to come back to the States."

"How's Jay-Jay holding up?"

"Okay I guess. Jay is kind of a wallflower. Though I hear all the work has caused him to loose weight, build some muscles. I feel kind of sorry for him. Don't you feel that way about Peg sometimes?"

"Now that you mention it," I realized with a start, "sometimes I do. I hate it when she lets the other kids give her a rough time about her figure. And she'd be so popular if only she'd lose a few pounds because she is so funny and so smart."

"Why is it teenagers can be so mean to one another?" Malcolm took a sip of his cola and cocked his head. "And why is it that all our all conversations get back to Jay-Jay or Peg? Tell you what, when Malcolm returns for his 'sabbatical', let's fix him and Peg up on a date. Until then, let's forget them and concentrate you, Saundra."

"Oh," my face heated. "There isn't much to tell. I've lived here all my live. My family likes to travel and I've been cross country to both the Pacific and Atlantic Oceans. Peg has been my best friend forever."

"No more Peg!" He ordered in mock ferocity.

"Sorry."

He wiped his lips and leaned toward me. His eyes stared so openly into mine. I felt intoxicated, like I had champagne fizzing all through my body.

"Gee, Saundra, you are so pretty, so much fun to talk to. What are you doing next Friday night?"

"Nothing," I whispered, as my whole body turned to mush. "Nothing at all."

"Well then you now have plans," he said abruptly, "Do you bowl?"

"Are you challenging me?" I took up on his playful mood, tossing down my used paper napkin like a gauntlet. "'Cause if you are, it seems I've knocked down a pin or two in my time."

"You're on." He laughed, again reaching for my hand.

As I'd expected by Thursday afternoon, Peg was wondering what junk food we should gather for our weekly gabfest.

"My Aunt insists that fruit and unbuttered popcorn are infinitely better than candy bars and soda. Would you mind if I stocked up on those instead of our usual, Saundra?"

Although I knew deep in my heart I should level with Peg, I simply couldn't bring myself to do it. She was so trusting and had such a huge crush on Malcolm.

"You know," she mused ignoring my silence, "if I could get Malcolm to kiss me I could literally have my cake and eat it, too. Just thin—his chocolate flavored kisses with absolutely no calories."

She laughed out loud at her own joke, assuming I would join her. When I didn't, she touched my sleeve.

"Hey Buddy, you okay?"

"Yeah, yeah. Listen," I was sweating, anxious to come clean. But like always when I looked at her innocent face, I lost my nerve. "Sorry, I won't be able to come over Friday night."

"Why not?"

I couldn't think fast enough so I gave the first excuse out of my head. It was a mistake.

"I'm babysitting for the Petersons."

"Alone—all three of them?"

"Hmmm, sure why not? Mrs. Peterson plans to have them all in bed before she and Mr. Peterson leave."

"Man, that will be a first." Peg smirked, rightly so.

After a second's thought though, she shrugged. "Why don't I come over anyway? I'm sure they wouldn't mind. I'll call her and ask."

"NO! NO!" I fairly shouted, overwrought to hide my lie. "I mean. That's not necessary. My niece is coming along so I can teach her proper babysitting techniques."

"Your niece," Peg shot me such a disbelieving face. "She's only 10. She's way too young to babysitting triplets!"

"Oh, I'm just showing her the ropes. Look, Peg, I've got to go or I'll be late for class. I'll see you later."

I spun on my heels and ran down the hall. Undoubtedly, my actions shocked Peg as much as they did me.

It wasn't easy not bumping into Peg again, but I managed that as well. The guilt I felt was maddening. I had trouble concentrating on my classes, and was even late for two of them as I took round about

94

routes to just to avoid my best friend. The stress of my lies were backing up and really messing with my head. Still, it seemed better to suffer this way than to tell the truth—cut to the quick my best friend. I hated doing it and more importantly, hated myself for not being truthful. I could only imagine how fine, upright Malcolm would feel if he knew what a horrible friend I was turning out to be.

And I couldn't even think about how Peg would react when she discovered my betrayal.

Of course at that time, I didn't realize that I didn't have much time to wait for the other shoe to drop.

"I thought you said you could bowl?" Malcolm teased me as we sat in the bowling alley's café sipping cokes and sharing a plate of nachos after our game.

"Oh anyone can have an off night." I giggled, shoving a cheese-loaded chip into his mouth.

The gooey cheese dripped down my fingers in a messy display. Suddenly, the smile on Malcolm's face softened as he gently wrapped his fingers around my wrist. Slowly, he began to lick the yellow stuff from my hand, his tongue cleaning my cuticles, my knuckles. Somehow he pulled me closer still until our noses were only millimeters apart. Once my hands were cleared of edible smudge, his eyes held mine and we both seemed to hold our breathe.

"Oh, Saundra," he whispered, his glance grazing my upturned face longingly. "You are such a darling person and I just want to be with you morning, noon and night."

I moistened my lips knowing he was going to kiss me. Of their own accord my eyes fluttered shut and my chin lifted in readiness. As our lips met, I felt as if the world had suddenly stopped twirling on its axis and time stood still. And though it wasn't a long, lingering kiss, it was a perfect first kiss. One that I knew I would cherish for my entire life.

But my enviable reverie was instantly shattered when I heard Peg's unmistakable voice cut into our second kiss.

"Well, isn't this cozy!"

"Hey Peg!" Malcolm grinned, misty traces of young love glowed on his face. "How are you?"

My own eyes flashed open and instantly I knew exactly how she was. She was furious and deeply hurt.

"Hi Peg," I could hardly look at her.

"You lying, backstabbing…How dare you? How dare you snatch Malcolm away from me with your skinny hips and soulful eyes. How could you do this to me, Saundra?"

I jumped up from my chair and for once, didn't even notice that Malcolm was in the room. "I'm sorry Peg. I didn't mean to. I was going to tell you, but every time I tried…"

"Save your lies you, two-faced heifer. I can't believe how you've treated me, your best friend!"

"I didn't betray you, Peg," I grabbed her arm, wanting wholeheartedly to explain, exonerate my deceit. "Please Peg!"

But she wouldn't listen and I didn't blame her. I knew exactly how she felt and why—because I would have felt the same way, too. Double-crossed, maligned and horribly exposed.

For a scant heartbeat, Peg just stood there glaring. Though he was totally in the dark about the situation, Malcolm did his best to soothe Peg and understand me. But his efforts were to no avail. Peg was steaming and everybody in the crowded place was watching. This time when I opened my mouth to speak, say anything that could fix this debacle, Peg picked up the oily yellow goop that I'd been feeding Malcolm. With an aim strong and true, she smeared the cheesy substance onto the top of my head, then dragged her slimy fingers across my face and neck.

"How could you treat me, your best friend, like this? Oh Saundra!" Her chubby emotional face trembled and tears glistened in her eyes. With the speed of light, she turned and ran out of the bowling alley. When I attempted to run after her, Malcolm caught my arm.

"Let her cool down a little, Saundra, while you explain to me what is going on."

Though I certainly didn't deserve his thoughtfulness, he signaled the waitress for a damp clothe and methodically, as I sat hiccupping, he wiped off my face and hair. His very tenderness was my undoing. Suddenly, all the frustration and fears and tears I'd been harboring over this incredible situation burst forth in a torrid explosion. I told him how Peg and I had developed crushes on him and how I hadn't wanted to hurt her or deny myself the pleasure of my first love.

"Now she has every right to hate me and so do you. I'm sorry, Malcolm. I never meant to put you in the middle of this and I definitely didn't mean to hurt her."

"I know, Saundra. And in time, I'm sure Peg will understand that too."

"I doubt it."

Despite my sniffly, puffy face and hair that wreaked of nachos, Malcolm walked me home, his arm wrapped comforting arm around my shoulders. We didn't speak. At my front door, he gave me tiny peck on the cheek and promised to call the next day.

He kept his promise. He even encouraged me to see Peg and make amends. And to my intense astonishment, he made arrangements for us to go to another movie Sunday afternoon, asking that I bring Peg.

"Fat chance of that happening. I'm going to be really lucky if she ever talks with me again."

"Stranger things have happened." I could feel his upbeat grin cuddle me over the phone.

After several failed attempts I finally got Peg to agree to let me come over. Quickly that afternoon, I made a big batch of brownies, which I knew she loved and then walked solemnly over to her house. It was obvious that she was still upset and angry.

"Here, I made you some of your favorite brownies, Peg."

"Why? So I can remain big and fat? Offer no hindrance to the men in your life—men that should be mine!"

"Oh Peg! You know that isn't true. You love brownies and I never meant—I never intended for some guy to come between us. You're my best friend forever. And the pressure of carrying on a double life is just killing me. I got caught up in that phenomenal flush of my first romance. Malcolm is such a great guy—you love him too. But, honestly, our friendship is more important to me—I'll tell him to get lost."

"Oh," she sneered, hands on hips, mouth pursed. "He says it was his fault. That he didn't realize that I had a crush on him and that by complimenting me so much, he didn't mean to lead me on."

"You've spoken with Malcolm?"

"Yes, he came by earlier today, to explain. He's very apologetic." Oddly, she shrugged her shoulders and made a typically silly Peg face. "And he's absolutely crazy about you."

"He is?"

"Of course, any idiot can see that even a jealous one."

Somehow, we looked at each other and it was like a huge cloud had lifted. Suddenly, we were hugging each other and laughing and talking all at once. We had a real heart to heart, the kind I'd been missing most.

"You think we can be friends again?" I asked, "Can you forgive me?"

"Well I could if you'd only notice—I've lost 8 pounds."

"Oh, Peg!" I studied her closely, "you have. How wonderful."

"Yes, I'm proud of myself. Besides, Malcolm says his cousin, Jay-Jay, is back and that if you and I will just forgive and forget, he'll arrange a double date for us this weekend."

"No kidding?"

"No kidding!" We hugged tightly. "Best Buds forever. Now let's have some brownies."

THE END

THE SWEETEST TABOO
Engaged . . .But Caught Between Two Lovers!

The first time I saw Paul, I knew he was the man for me. I was walking down the street to meet my girls for breakfast and there he was—looking so handsome, I actually stumbled. But just like the Prince Charming that he turned out to be, he was right there by my side and caught me before I fell. From that moment on, we were nearly inseparable.

Paul took me out to dinner that night, and he told me all about himself. He was a schoolteacher. He taught middle school English at a private school. He had a dream of becoming principal one day.

I know that might sound boring to some, but to me, it was music to my ears. Having grown up in a neighborhood where so many of the men aspired to be the biggest baller on the block, Paul's desire to make it legitimately was such a turn-on to me, I could hardly contain myself. When I shared with him that I was a nail tech—not at a nail salon, but at a high-class spa—he didn't look down on me or anything. He just smiled and said he'd love to have a manicure one day.

For months, I spent so much time with Paul, that my girls thought I was neglecting them. They accused me of kicking them to the curb for a man and all kinds of craziness like that. But the fact was, I had been spending more and more time with Paul. Even when I was with my girls, I was talking about Paul or thinking about him. So, when he finally asked me to marry him, I was the happiest woman alive.

We decided on a six-month engagement. And six months was about as long as I could stand. Inside, I felt like I couldn't wait another minute to be Mrs. Paul Douglas.

On the day after I announced my engagement, my girls took me out for an evening on the town. They wanted to treat me to something special, so we went to an upscale supper club in downtown Tulsa. The club was famous for exquisite food and first-class entertainment. We placed our orders and waited for the show to begin. If I had known then that my love life would change forever, I might have had second thoughts about going out that night.

As the lights went down in the chic establishment, men and women in black and white uniforms served us plates of food with names I'd heard of only on television, but never once thought I would

98

ever eat. I took a bite and moaned at the exquisite blend of seasonings coming to life in my mouth. I thought I was in heaven. And then the most seductive man I'd ever seen took the stage, and I learned what a true slice of heaven was.

He was introduced as Julian Knight, and he sat on a stool in the middle of a stage that looked like it could accommodate an entire band. I expected other musicians to join him onstage, but he was alone, and he was magnificent. All he did was play the guitar, but he played the strings so masterfully, I started to imagine that it wasn't the strings he was plucking, but the most sensitive parts of my body.

Before I knew it, my food was cold, but my body was hot. He had me in a spell that it would take a miracle for me to break out of.

My girls, Faleesa and Dee, noticed me checking him out right away.

"Girl, slow your roll!"

"Yeah, Brina. You're undressing him with your eyes."

"And he looks good naked!" I told them.

In my mind, and in reality, he did. Light brown hair, skin the color of peanut butter, amber warm eyes, and the brightest white teeth I'd ever seen. He wore a sleeveless shirt and his biceps tightened and relaxed with the rhythm of his guitar. He played haunting Spanish melodies that made me feel like I'd dipped myself in a vat of sangria. I didn't know an instrument—or a man playing one—could be so intoxicating.

Before the end of the night, I noticed his eyes on me all smoky and smoldering. I was glad Paul wasn't around to see me, because I made it obvious that I found Julian attractive. Very, very attractive.

At one point, I was so excited by his performance, that I excused myself from the table, went to the ladies room and splashed cold water on my face. I looked in the mirror and didn't recognize the reflection I saw. I was ashamed. I was engaged, and I had just begun plans to get married in six months. The way I was staring at that man was shameless. Paul, my fiancé, was a good man—a decent man with decent ways. The things I was thinking about Julian were . . . .

Brazen.

As I exited the bathroom, someone fell instep behind me, and grabbed me by the waist.

Startled, I made a move to see who it was. The voice I heard, made my heart beat double-time in my chest.

"Don't," the voice said. "Don't turn around."

"Who are you? What do you want?"

"You know who I am, and you know what I want."

Julian's lips were inches from my ear. The hot breath from his mouth settled against my skin and made me tingle in the darkened hallway.

His strong body guided me to the side and into what was obviously a dressing room.

Once we got inside, I no longer needed to turn around. In the wall-to-wall mirror, I saw myself wrapped against Julian's tall luxurious body.

Everything inside my mind shouted, "No!" but my body knew exactly what it wanted.

Julian lips brushed against my bare shoulder, then he placed a slow kiss on my neck. The moan that escaped my lips surprised me. I had never done anything like this before. But I didn't want him to stop.

"Your eyes called me from across the room," he said.

His voice was so low and so sexy, if he had asked me to strip naked and spread my legs, I would have done just that. But he didn't. Instead, he did the most erotic thing possible.

He stopped, let me go, and left me wanting. He told me he wanted to see me again, and then he went back to finish his set at the supper club.

That night when I left with my girls, I went home to Paul throbbing wet. In our bedroom, Paul reached for me, but I told him I was too tired. Truth was, I knew there was nothing he could do to me right then that would top the sensation of Julian's guitar-playing hands on my body.

The worst thing that man could have done was to leave me hanging and desperately wanting more. But that's just what he'd done, and I closed my eyes determined to get it.

The week after I went to the supper club, Faleesa and Dee went back there with me. They knew I was fascinated with the musician, but out of respect, they didn't tease me about it too much. They probably thought that I had a mild infatuation with the man. But already, it was more than that. He was a temptation I had to experience for myself. But just once, I told myself.

I loved Paul, and I had no interest in having a long sordid affair. Just a one-time thing—just to see if the man could do to a woman the same thing he did to a guitar. After that, my life with Paul would be business as usual; at least that's what I thought.

But already, my behavior was changing. I went to see Julian's show every week for a month. He was a regular at the club. I had to go without my friends. I didn't want them to suspect that I was hooked on seeing a man that I didn't even know. His sexy mesmerizing music possessed my lust long before his body ever did. And every performance night, during intermission, I would meet Julian in his dressing room and he would kiss me until I couldn't see straight.

To cover up my indiscretion, I would stop at a convenience store on the way home, ask for a cup of ice, and use the frozen cubes to ease the swelling of my lips. I didn't want Paul to know that some other man had kissed me so deep with passion that my lips were engorged.

In all this time, my desire to be with Paul had diminished. I can't explain it. It was like, the more I saw of Julian, the less I wanted to be with Paul. My fiancé thought I was out making wedding arrangements, but in reality, I was out enjoying the caress of another man.

Paul hadn't complained about the lack of loving yet, but I could tell by his intense stares and quiet demeanor, that he would if I didn't relent. So one night, I did, and while Paul kissed and caressed me, I imagined the face and body of a guitar player. I wanted Julian more than ever.

The next time I went to the supper club, Julian was in rare form. Our eyes locked on to each other's, and they stayed that way for his entire first set. He played with a passion so exquisite, I could feel it stirring between my legs.

That night during intermission, he wouldn't let me back into his dressing room. He said he wanted me so badly that if I came in, he would take me right then and there, and spend so much time making love to me that he would miss the rest of his set. Instead, he told me to meet him out back after the show, and he would show me something.

I couldn't wait. Even though I loved his playing, his performance was a blur until I met Julian in the alley.

"I'm going to finally give you what you want," he said, pressing me up against a dank building wall. It was dark—so dark, I could barely make out the shapes of buildings, the abandoned car, or our own silhouettes in the filtered moonlight.

He held my arms above my head. The sensation was so thrilling, I can barely describe it. In the years Paul and I had been together, I had never cheated on him. The thrill of Julian as something forbidden and erotic made my juices flow like a rushing river.

"Kiss me," I said.

He took my mouth as if our lips were created for just that moment. We shared a kiss so searing and intense, I forgot I had a man.

"Let's go to your place," I moaned.

He pressed his hard body on mine, pushing me flat against the wall. The passion in his eyes ignited like liquid fire. "No. Here."

"Here?"

After that, we stopped talking. It was as if we had both lost our minds and in a forgotten part of the city, we stripped naked, and we made love standing up until the dark night filled with our cries of pleasure.

Julian was a good lover. After that night, I always brought a change of clothes with me. There was no telling where we would do it. In a park, by the river, in a cab. No matter where we were in public, if we were sitting next to each other, Julian's hand was always discreetly up my skirt fingering me. I got very good at coming quietly, and biting my lip to keep for screaming his name.

One time, I thought we were actually going to go to his apartment and make love on his bed. We only got as far as the landing in his third floor walk up. At three a.m. when I had told my fiancé that I was having a late night out with the girls, I had multiple thrills in the stairwell of Julian's apartment building. It was the most erotic act I had performed in my entire life.

All of my thoughts of a one-night stand with Julian were long gone. I couldn't get him out of my system. I was consumed with touching him and being touched by him.

I'd been seeing Julian for four months, and during that whole time, Paul never questioned me about anything. But then again, Paul never would. He wasn't like some of the men I'd grown up with who would have been in my face about who I was with and where I was going. No. Paul was too dignified for that. But he must have sensed that something was wrong. I was hardly ever home, and we didn't make love nearly as often.

One day, when I was missing Julian like crazy, Paul suggested we go away together—for a weekend, or maybe an extended weekend. He said that he had an in-service break coming up. The kids would be out of school for a few days. He wanted us to go somewhere. He suggested a romantic getaway in New Mexico or Montana. Not only did I disagree with his choice of locations, but the thought of being away from Julian that long made me sick to my stomach.

"Paul, baby. Do you really think that's such a good idea with the wedding coming up? We're going to need every penny just to break even."

While I stacked the dinner plates in the dishwasher, Paul came up behind me, and he turned me around. For a moment, I thought of Julian. He had no problems handling me the way I wanted to be handled. This was the first time Paul touched me without being the perfect gentleman.

"Brina, what's wrong? We've been acting like strangers for months."

"Nothing's wrong," I said. I couldn't look directly at him. If I did, I thought he would see Julian's kisses all over me, his fingerprints all over me, his passion all inside me.

"You would tell me, right?" Paul asked, grasping my arms, pulling me closer. "You would tell me if something was . . . wrong?"

I could smell his cologne. He'd worn the same scent for years. Old Spice. And that was exactly what Paul was. Old school. Old-fashioned. He was the old spice in my life, Julian was the new flavor, and I had a taste for both. I didn't see how I could give either of them up. But I smiled as if there were no Julian, and I looked my fiancé in the eye. His face brightened and he returned my smile.

"How are we doing on detergent?" he asked.

"Huh?" I replied, not understanding.

"For the dishes. You said earlier that we were low." He ran a finger across my cheek, smoothing back a stray hair.

"Oh, yeah," I said, surprised at how such a subtle gesture could affect me. "We need some."

"Then I'll be right back," he said, and left me standing in a state of confusion. How could I want two men? And then, I decided. I had to end this thing with Julian. I would be married soon anyway. How can I continue to see him when I would be a married woman?

I grabbed my purse and hurried out the door. I was determined to find Julian, break it off with him, and get home before Paul returned.

I started down the hallway of my apartment building and two words stopped me in my tracks. "Hey, Momma."

I would know Julian's dark chocolate voice, anywhere. His sound was the color of night, and it was implanted on me, forever. I spun around, shocked.

"Julian? How did you . . . what are you doing here?"

He strolled toward me. "I couldn't stand being away from you. Standing on the other side of this wall is better than being alone in my apartment."

"Julian," I stammered. "There's something I need to tell you. I can't . . . ."

"I know," he said, closing the gap between us. "You can't stand being away from me either."

He enveloped me in his arms, and there in front of God and all my neighbors, we kissed like passion-starved lovers.

"Let's go inside," I breathed, surprising myself. I was offering my lover my fiancé's bed.

"No," he said. "Come on."

He took my hand, and together, we hurried to a coffee shop around the corner. We trotted toward the back corridor where the restrooms were, and we went inside the women's.

"Julian. . . . "

He placed a finger over his lips, and I waited in silence while he checked the stalls. There was no one inside but us. Quickly, he locked the door, and we reached for each other, frenzied by the abandon of intense need. All my thoughts of breaking it off with Julian left my head as soon as his hand found my soft moist spot, and he massaged me until I cried. We didn't bother taking our clothes off. We just got naked enough so that he could put on a condom and thrust inside me.

He pinned me to the door and rocked me to the core. I clung to him, panting like the crazed woman I was. I couldn't stop. No matter what. As we humped hard toward ecstasy, I didn't think that even my marriage could keep me away from Julian and the pleasure he gave me.

Suddenly, it was too much pleasure.

"Julian, I have to go."

"No you don't," he said.

I straightened my clothes. "Yes, I do."

For two months, I focused on my wedding. Julian and I didn't see each other, and I thought he was out of my life.

But on my wedding day, I found out I was wrong. While Faleesa and Dee helped me get ready, there was a knock on my door.

"I'll get it," Dee offered. "When I heard her say, "Ooh . . ." I knew why immediately.

"Can I come in?" Julian's voice melted me like chocolate. But I knew it would be for the last time.

"It's okay," I said, and my girls stepped out to give me some alone time with a man who could play every inch of my body they way he played a guitar.

"I came to give you a wedding present."

"Julian—" I began, but before I could finish my sentence, he opened his hand and in his palm was a key. The metal shone in the light of the room. It was the key to his apartment. After months of wanting to make love to Julian in his bed, he was finally offering me what I wanted for so long. I could come and go as I pleased.

I turned away. I couldn't continue to see Julian. And what was more important, I didn't want to. I had everything I needed in Paul. And it took being with Julian, and then being away from him to make me realize that.

"I don't want your key, Julian—not anymore."

He came up behind me and wrapped his arms around my waist just like he did the first time in the supper club.

"Then let me give you something to remember me by."

I closed my eyes, and I braced myself against the back of a chair. Julian found his way through my simple wedding dress, lifted it, and he took me quickly, thoroughly. I kept my eyes closed. This time, visions of Julian mixed with visions of Paul—until the only one left was Paul.

I couldn't wait to get married.

When we finished, Julian readjusted my dress, and he zipped himself up. We looked like two people who had just shared a cup of coffee, instead of two people who had quenched the final fires of lust between them.

Julian walked to the door and stopped before walking out. "Take care, Momma," he said.

"I will," I responded, but he was already gone, and I was already putting my lust far behind me and focusing on the man I loved. A man I would love and be faithful to from now on . . . .

THE END

FORBIDDEN ECSTASY
For one night, my married lover
was all mine!

The going-away party was over, and all the people from the department had said good-bye and good luck and all that to me. I was elated at the prospect of moving up to something better, and all the well-wishers had buoyed my spirits. The challenge of the unknown made me a little fearful. I had my own personal reason to feel a little sad, too, but hopeful.

Up until this morning the reason had been purely fantasy and hadn't worked and couldn't have; I couldn't even mention it to anyone before this. I still couldn't, really. I had to act, not talk. For four long years, I had kept hoping and had tried to act happy, although I had felt in my heart that it was hopeless. Now, since this morning, I had one slim but compelling reason to be hopeful—Harry Jackson.

Harry Jackson, my boss—my former boss, as of two hours ago—came back from paying for the hot hors d'oeuvres. He was fine. He was a delicious-looking man. Beautiful features with the most seductive eyes I had ever seen. Harry also took care of himself, and I liked that. No fat. All lean, streamlined, sexy muscle. I'd had my eye on him since Day One.

"Well, Roxy, how does it feel to be done with your last day of slave labor?" he joked.

"Not bad, Harry, not bad. Real good in fact. But slaving for you hasn't been so bad, either. You've been a really good boss."

"You mean that, Roxanne? I appreciate hearing it one-on-one. You praised me to high heaven in your thank-you-and-good-bye speech just now. But everybody does, after all."

"I do mean it, Harry," I said with some feeling.

As he reached down to get his folds of speech notes off the table, he asked, "How come you're still here? I see everybody leaving. I thought—"

"I need a ride. Pattie left already, and I came with her."

"She stood you up, did she?"

"No, not really. She had too much to drink, and I convinced her to ride with someone else and get her car later. She went with Gordon."

"Ah, yes, Gordon. The department's one and only bachelor!"

"Why, Harry, you sound jealous!" I teased.

"No, no Roxy. I'm a happily married man."

I knew better, but I answered, "I know, Harry. That's such a nice family picture you have on your desk." And it was. His boy was eight or so, and away at a boarding school. His wife was a sort of mousy little woman, but smiling in the picture. Harry, himself, was young and handsome—the youngest department head in the whole corporation, I had heard. Then I reiterated, "I need a ride."

"Would you like to come with me? Where can I take you?"

Relieved that he finally caught on, I answered, "Love to, Harry—thanks. Back to the office. I remembered a couple of things I forgot to take."

"Okay, let's go," he urged, putting his hand on my shoulder momentarily to turn me in the direction of the door. He dropped his hand almost immediately, but it had felt good for that short moment.

We got our coats and went on out to Harry's car. It was a brand-new four-door model, conservative—a perfect family car. Harry opened the door and held it for me. As I slithered in, I think he was looking at the deep slit in the front of my skirt, but when I looked up to smile and thank him, his eyes were already turned away.

Then he got in on his side, and he insisted that I buckle my seat belt. So conservative, even for a ride of only a few blocks.

On the ride back from the cocktail lounge he hardly said a word, concentrating on the turns and traffic lights and stop signs. The traffic was still fairly heavy that Friday evening, with some people still heading home and others going out already.

In the office I went to hang up my coat on the rack with his, but he stopped me.

"You can't do that," he reminded me. "The company won't allow employees to keep men's and women's clothing together. You know that."

"Oh, come on," I retorted, "nobody will see! Everyone has left. The secretaries' closet is way down the hall, and I'll only be a minute. Besides, I'm not part of the company anymore."

"But I am," Harry retorted, "and I have to live by the regulations. It's all part of Equal Employment Opportunity and not harassing women and all. I work strictly by the book."

I was getting my stuff out of my desk drawers, but I kept on talking. "That's one of the things I've liked about you as a boss, Harry. You haven't done one single thing or said one single solitary word to harass me all this time. You certainly aren't one of these fanny-patters like some guys around here."

As I said that, I leaned over to reach a bottom drawer. He was standing right behind me, so he had to get the picture.

As I stood up and turned around to face him, Harry got a very serious look on his face and asked me, "Do you really want to know how far I've had to go with this fanny-patting thing, Roxanne?"

"Tell me," I said, wondering what would come next.

"Do you remember Paul?" he asked.

"Sure."

"Well, he's gone and you're leaving for Houston so I can tell you. I had to fire him for sexual harassment in the workplace. Words—and actions, too. He wouldn't stop when warned, so I documented it all and went by the book and fired him. He was one of my best supervisors, but I fired him. We kept it all very cordial and smooth, and nobody knew."

"I had an idea," I said.

"The grapevine?" he asked.

"More than that. He tried a little persuasion on me once."

"That dirty dog!" spat Harry vehemently in righteous indignation. I thought I could sense something in his voice—maybe envy.

With only a moment's hesitation he asked, "What did he do? You didn't report it at the time."

"He said he could get me a job as of an inspector on the production line which paid pay more than secretary. He

just wanted a little session out in his car."

"Did you?" asked Harry before he could catch himself.

"I stayed on as your secretary, didn't I?" I answered. I wasn't about to tell Harry one way or the other. Let him imagine. Besides, he knew Paul never had the power to fulfill a promise like that.

Harry quickly changed the subject and asked, "Are you ready? I'll walk you to your car. The parking lot is kind of dark."

"My car's not here. I rode in with Pattie, too. I'll call a cab."

"Oh! No, don't! I'll drive you. May I?" he asked politely.

"Please. That would be great. But don't put yourself out."

"No problem. Where's your car? In the shop?"

"No, at my apartment. I have a trailer hooked on behind, and I'm leaving in the morning, first thing," I explained.

"Leaving so soon? And driving all by yourself?" he asked.

"Sure. I've got to get to my next job. I've got something really nice lined up. Executive secretary to a VP in an oil company. My uncle in Texas arranged some good interviews."

By this time we were at his car, and he let me in politely. I was sure he looked up my skirt again.

On the drive over to my apartment complex I picked up on the topic of harassment again.

"Do you remember that van I had when I joined your department; the one my ex had left me with when I got divorced?" I asked. "The one with the high step to get into the cab?"

"Vaguely," he murmured.

"Well, another of your fellows—I won't say who—saw me getting

107

out of it one day. I had on one of my slit skirts, and despite the slit I had to pull the skirt up to make the step. He leered—which is perfectly normal—" I paused before I continued. "But when I came out later in the day I found the words FOXY ROXY printed in big, bold letters in the dust on the side of the van. I'm almost certain he did it."

"Typical, typical," said Harry, somewhat agitated.

"Oh, I could tell you lots of juicy ones," I chortled.

"Too bad there's no time," he said in a voice, which seemed to show a little bit of longing. "We're up to your complex. Where do I pull in?"

I showed him, and he stopped in a visitors' parking spot. Before he could open his mouth, I asked, "Harry, could I possible impose upon you to do me a favor? I have a bureau to put into the trailer, which is too heavy for me to carry down the stairs alone, and my next-door neighbor, who promised earlier, bailed out this morning. Would you help me?"

"Sure, but how come? I thought these were furnished apartments."

"They are, but they give you the absolute minimum—stove, refrigerator, dinette set, one bureau, one bed, one couch, one floor lamp. I've got stuff leftover from before, and I picked up a couple more things last year. Including this bureau."

"Fine. We'll move it."

"Won't your wife mind if you're home so late?"

"She's not home," he told me.

"Now why did I ask that? I knew that already!" I exclaimed in mock dismay.

"How did you—" he began.

"I took the phone call, Harry. I gave you the number to call her back."

"Right! So you did! She's visiting her mother in Atlanta," he told me.

"Is it Atlanta?" I asked, knowing perfectly well that it was. I had checked. Then I continued, "She must go a lot. I've gotten that area code from her before when she's called you."

"She goes a lot," he returned glumly. I thought I sensed a touch of anger in his voice.

"She calls you a lot at work, too," I continued. "It must be nice to be so close and loving."

But, I thought to myself: Sure, loving. I've heard the acid in her voice almost every time she's called you over the last four years. Even when she'd just ask, "Is Harry there?" I could sense it. She can't hide it. Why do you endure it? You're just too nice.

So caught up in my thoughts, I had barely heard his answer. "Yes, we try to be a perfect couple," he said.

If you have to try, you've failed already. But it can't be your fault, Harry, I thought. From what little I know of you, it can't possibly be your fault.

However, I answered quickly, "Gee, that's great. But let's get on upstairs and move the bureau, Harry."

In the vestibule I slipped off my coat and carried it as I went up the stairs ahead of Harry. I knew just what level his eyes were at, and I emphasized my walk just a little bit.

In the apartment, I let him drop his coat across a chair, and then I draped mine on top of his. I made sure he noticed. Then I went over to the dresser and began to pull out the drawers to make it lighter to carry. My stuff was still in them—why pack since my new apartment was waiting for me?—and I stacked the drawers on the floor.

Harry helped me. I made sure he got to pull out the drawer with my lingerie last, and put it on top of the stack. Right out on top was one of my bikini panties with the lacy transparent front panels, on top on purpose. The drawer was perfumed, too.

After the last load, I offered Harry a drink from my bottle of bourbon, which I hadn't packed yet, and he accepted. He sipped several as we sat there on the couch, him on the left and me on the right, not very far away. I was sitting side-saddle, almost facing him, with my left heel up under me. I had pulled up my skirt enough to get comfortable. Harry kept glancing down.

He talked a lot about how well we had worked together—how I had gotten reports out on time, and kept his calendar perfectly, and gotten his coffee without his ever asking—even the first time so he wouldn't be accused of harassment. This, I could see, touched him deeply, and I bet myself that he had to pour his own at home. But that was over, I knew.

That phone call today—it had been Atlanta, all right, but not his wife or his mother. It had been a very professional secretary, and when I had said that Mr. Jackson was out she had left a curt message and phone number.

I had then called back and gotten a receptionist—not the same secretary—who had given the firm's name. It was one of those that sounds like "Paint, Plaster, Varnish and Turpentine." Well, I had asked for Mr. Turpentine, and I had faked a story about contemplating a divorce, and Mr. Turpentine had said it was their specialty. Then, under an AKA, I had made an appointment, had thanked Mr. Turpentine very much and hung up.

My message to Harry had just been to call his wife at the number that had been left. Harry had called back, so he knew it was a lawyer's officer. He knew the score.

As I was thinking this, Harry was still talking on and on about how well we had worked together That idea, that word, "together, together, together," kept coming through.

Now, I thought, right now, at last. You're ready and so am I.

I put my left hand behind his and pulled his head down and leaned around and kissed him. I held on and pulled harder. I felt his lips against mine, and my head began to swim. We were finally going to. . . .

Suddenly, he pushed me away. He pushed me away! It was all over. All my waiting for four years, all my planning tonight—all over! Suddenly, I got so mad I could spit! I felt like slapping him right across the mouth. He was holding me at arm's length by the shoulders, holding me away. I would have broken away and hauled back and hit him, too, except that I looked into his face just then. Harry was totally down. His face drooped and his brow was furrowed. Even more, his eyes held sadness and terror.

"My wife—" he mumbled.

Then, I knew. I read his heart. My anger melted, and I blurted out, "Harry, you poor guy. You've been a slave for so long!"

This startled him, and he looked at me quizzically.

I didn't finish the sentence, though. I didn't say: But today, you are free! He had to come up with that. He had to realize it, and turn himself loose.

I could see his mind working. He scowled, then raised one eyebrow, then cocked his head over to the other side. Then he looked me straight in the eye. Both his eyebrows went up and a little grin appeared at the corners of his mouth. The grin spread. It was the happiest smile I had ever seen. He had figured it out!

"You're better than a lawyer!" he almost shouted.

He squeezed me together with his strong arms. His grin turned to longing, and he pulled me to him and enveloped me with those arms I adored.

I flung my arms around his neck, pulling him down to kiss him some more. A great wave of expectation washed over me. He kissed ferociously but was gentle at the same time. Soon his hands were all over me. He made good use of the deep slit in my skirt, and I clung to him—oh, so tightly! I had wanted this for so long—indeed, for four years, ever since I had met him at my interview. But he was a company man, and a good family man—but, today he was free!

I held him tight a little while longer as he got his hand inside the back of my blouse and unhooked my bra. Then I sat up a little straighter and began to undress him. He did the same for me. We stood up for the last items, and I turned in the direction of the bedroom. Before I could take a step, Harry grabbed me and held me at arm's length by the shoulders and looked me up and down.

Standing, he shook his head very slightly and very slowly from side to side as if to say, "My God, how beautiful," or, "Is this really for me?" I wanted to scream, "Yes, Harry, it's for you! Take it! Take me!" but I just smiled at him.

Then he loosened his grip and ran his hands all over me, time and again. I let him, wanting even more. As he touched, he had a look near reverence on his face. Then he grabbed me and pulled me to him and held me tight and kissed me ferociously. I pushed up against him as closely as I could and felt the heat rising from his body.

Finally I led him to the bedroom, where he took his time to satisfy me. And it didn't take much time, either. I had been wanting him all evening, all day, all week, all year—four years. In our situation there had been no way for even a wink or a grin. And now, perfection.

At last—Harry Jackson is mine! I thought happily.

Rapture engulfed me. The world disappeared, and Harry and I were one. It was the greatest experience I had ever had. Beyond this, I could sense it was good for Harry, too; he shook and moaned and twitched and almost squeezed the breath out of me.

We lay there a long, long time, and he still didn't say a word. Finally, when he did say how wonderful it had been at first, I didn't believe his words. They all say that. But then I did know that what he was saying was true, because I read his body language.

Harry stayed all night, what with his wife away and his boy being at that boarding school. Probably Harry was hoping for a session in the morning, and, I suppose, to delay me even longer. I wished I could, and would have loved to have been able to, but I had to leave. Besides, I don't like good-byes. I don't like scenes.

So, wishing I didn't have to, I got up very early while he was still sleeping like a log, and got ready to leave. I didn't even try to give him a peck on the cheek. No good-byes. For my good-bye, I left him a note. I wanted it to be more of a hello than a good-bye, and it was. It read:

Harry,

I think I could love you very much. I don't guarantee, but I think so. I'll call you and give you my number as soon as I get a phone. I'm leaving you the key to this apartment The rent is paid till the end of the month. You may want to stop in here and think about me. I know about the law office. If and when you get your life sorted out, please call. I'll let you know if my situation changes. I hope this is hello, not good-bye.

R.

That's how I signed it and that's how I left. I put the note and the key and also my transparent bikini panties—the pair I had been wearing yesterday—on the bed beside him, and left.

All day in the car I thought about him, remembering our lovemaking. I hoped he wanted to remember me, too—and more.

THE END

WAITING FOR
MR. RIGHT
I Knew He Would Come Back To Me!

"Vanessa! Over here!"

I turned in the direction of my friend, Takesha's, voice and saw her waving frantically at me. Since the diner was crowded, I'm glad she got here early enough to snare a table.

"Sorry, I'm late. Printer problems."

"Not a problem here. I even got us a table with a view."

The view was of the bathrooms, but with a half dozen people waiting on line to be seated, who was quibbling?

Takesha had been my best friend since I first knew what the word meant. We shared our dolls, tears and laughter growing up. Still close, we met at least once a week for lunch. We didn't work too far from one another, which made things easy. When she called me last night, she hinted that she had something totally out of sight to tell me. I assumed she met the man of her dreams—for this week, anyway. Takesha was the only girl I knew who could fall in and out of love so quickly. It seemed she changed boyfriends like underwear.

"So what was the earth-shattering news that you had to tell me?"

"Are you two gals ready to order?" the waitress interrupted.

It was amazing how they picked their moments, I mused. We ordered and she disappeared once more.

"Tell me quick before we get interrupted again," I half-pleaded.

"Tell you what?" Takesha asked, but I could tell from that half-smirk she was trying to hide that she was teasing. Suddenly the smirk became a full-blown smile. "You'll never guess who now works in the sales department of my ad agency."

"My crystal ball is in the repair shop. Can't you just tell me?"

"Tyrone Banks."

Just the sound of his name made me feel warm and fuzzy inside. I had such a major crush on him that began in junior high when he gave me my first kiss. He was such a hunk, even at fourteen. We were at a party playing spin the bottle and the bottle pointed to me. I thought I had died and went to heaven, refusing to wash my lips for days.

Takesha would often tease me about how I felt about Tyrone. "That torch you carry is like an eternal flame. Time to get over it, girlfriend." But, no matter who I dated, I never quite forgot that first kiss or the boy who gave it to me. Of course, even though we were in some of the same classes, he hardly knew I existed. He dated mainly cheerleaders. That didn't stop me from always wishing and hopping that he'd eventually realize that I was the one for him and ask me out. When he moved away two years later, I cried for a week. I never saw him again.

"Is that torch still burning?" Takesha chided.

"So, how does he look?"

"Older?"

"That's all you can say? I need details, girl."

"I could try and describe him or..."

"What?"

"You can see first hand for yourself."

The thought of seeing Tyrone Banks again set my pulse racing in high gear. "How do you intend to arrange that?"

"I'll come up with something," Takesha replied.

She sometimes scared me when she said that. Being somewhat of a daredevil, who not only thought out of the box but out of any known shape, she sometimes devised real doozies. We talked a little more before our sandwiches came and before we knew it, it was time to go back to work.

I found it hard to concentrate on my work. My mind kept wandering back to Tyrone Banks. It had been so many years ago, yet how could I forget how he looked when he smiled with those cute dimples? Or how his warm brown eyes were always twinkling? Then reality began to set in. Aside from not knowing I exist, he was probably happily married with a half-dozen kids. I hadn't even given that any thought and I should have, for I made it my business never to get involved with married men. That type of relationship reminded me of suicide, and like suicide, it had no future.

Takesha didn't disappoint me and managed to arrange for Tyrone and another salesman from the office to have lunch at our favorite diner. She called me with the time.

"This is your big moment, girlfriend."

"I wish. The guy probably doesn't remember me."

"Then you make certain that you remind him."

"Is he married?"

"You know something, I never noticed."

"It wouldn't matter, anyway. Many guys don't wear wedding rings."

"Tomorrow, then."

"Thanks, Takesha."

"No, problem, girlfriend."

That night I dreamt I was back in junior high again playing spin the bottle. Only, I was as old as I am now, twenty-six. Though I had grown up, Tyrone hadn't aged a day. I awoke wondering what the dream was supposed to mean.

The following morning I put on my favorite suit. No matter what, I wanted to look my best. I watched the hands on the clock as they slowly moved around its face until it was time to go to lunch. Even though, I got out earlier than usual, Takesha and the guys were already seated at a table waiting for me. I saw her wave, but my eyes were on the guys. Both men stood as I approached.

"Wesley Green, Tyrone Banks, this is my friend, Vanessa Summers."

My eyes were on Tyrone. He was simply the most beautiful man I'd ever seen. I felt a catch in my throat. And when he shook hands with me, I felt a surge of excitement travel straight through me to my very core.

"Takesha tells me that we all went to school together. It's nice to see you again," he said, but I could tell that he didn't remember me. But the big blow came when I noticed that he was wearing a wedding band. Perhaps I should take Takesha's advice and move on, even though I always felt there was a chance that we'd end up together one day.

As we talked about school and traded memories, I found myself envying the woman who had captured Tyrone's heart and had given him a beautiful little girl. Time fled to wherever it goes when you're enjoying yourself and we all agreed to have lunch again together.

"I'm glad you and Wesley hit it off," I told Takesha later on that night.

"Too bad, things didn't go according to plan for you, as well, Vanessa."

"That's okay. I'd rather be Tyrone's friend and see him from time to time, than not at all."

"But, promise me that you'll date others and not pine over him."

"I'm not becoming a nun, if that's what you're thinking."

"That's my girl," Takesha said and we hung up.

That Saturday I went food shopping at the supermarket. I really hated to food shop and tried to get in and out as quickly as possible. I was rushing around the corner when I nearly whacked into a cart that was coming from the other side.

It turned out to be Tyrone. He was doing his own food shopping with his daughter, who was sitting in the seat. He noticed me first.

"Vanessa, what's up?"

"Oh, Tyrone. Hi. Sorry. I took that curve a little too quickly."

"Are you that reckless on the highway, too?" he kidded.

"I'm in practice. Who's that beautiful little girl?"

"That's Malika."

"I'm four!"

"Well, good for you."

"Mommy's home sleeping."

I nodded my head. I really had no reply to that, but because it was nearly eleven o'clock I did think Jasmine was a lucky woman to have her husband take care of her kid so she could sleep so late.

"Mommy should be getting up soon and she'll want milk to put in her coffee," he said to Malika. "We best be going."

"Nice meeting you, Malika. Bye, Tyrone."

I watched them walk away and finished my shopping. I truly loved kids and wanted to get married and have my own one day. Too bad the one man I always wanted was already taken.

Takesha began to date Wesley and they wanted to be alone every chance they got. That was okay by me, since Tyrone and I became really good friends. Seeing and speaking to him more, I began to detect a note of unhappiness, though. He wasn't as carefree as I once thought he was. He would often email me at home and we'd chat on line. I soon realized that he was alone by himself a great deal while his wife, Jasmine, went out with her friends. He never complained about it, but I could tell by the way he mentioned it that it really bothered him. If he really wanted me to know, he'd eventually tell me. Until then, I didn't question him.

Takesha and Tyrone both wanted me to come to their Christmas party. It was being catered at a nice restaurant down town. I had nothing else planned so I agreed to go.

In one of our email chats I happen to ask Tyrone, "Why aren't you taking your wife?"

"She didn't really think an office party was worth going to since she'd have to get a

sitter."

It didn't seem that Jasmine took an interest in anything that Tyrone did. I was beginning to really dislike her. And I hadn't even met the woman. No matter what Tyrone said, I knew he felt badly that Jasmine hadn't come. It turned out that he was the only married guy who'd come without his wife. Something had to be so wrong with his marriage.

At the party Tyrone headed for the bar, the first thing. He didn't nurse the drink, but belted it right down. I watched him down another just as quickly.

"Have something to eat," I suggested. "You don't want to get sick."

I saw a flash of anger in his eyes, but a smile followed it. "You're a good friend, Vanessa."

"I just care about you, Tyrone. And I want you to know I always will."

He drew me close and kissed my cheek. The spot on her cheek felt as if it had been branded. If only he knew how much I cared…

He didn't stop drinking, but did slow down on his intake. We got some stuff to eat from the buffet and found an empty table. In the middle of discussing our all-time favorite movies, Tyrone threw me a curve ball.

"You know, Shallow Hal was written for guys just like me."

"What do you mean?"

"I only wanted to date cheerleaders when I was younger. I even married that type of girl. But it's true what they say."

"What's that?"

"Beauty is only skin deep. It turns out that Jasmine was just as shallow as me."

"I'm truly sorry to hear that."

"Sometimes you don't recognize beauty until it's too late."

I was going to ask him what he meant, but got distracted. I sincerely hoped that he'd been referring to me. This was the first time he actually said anything bad about his wife. Before it had only been mere innuendos. Perhaps the drinks had loosened his tongue. I certainly hoped that he wouldn't feel bad about telling me when he thought about it tomorrow. As the night wore on, I became increasingly worried about him driving home, so I suggested we go for a walk outside in order to clear his head.

As we were walking, I tripped and would have tumbled to the ground, had Tyrone not caught me in his strong arms. In a moment of weakness, our eyes met and locked. Suddenly his mouth was on mine. This small taste of his sweet lips wasn't nearly enough for me. I needed more and found myself returning the kiss with all the pent-up passion I felt. Then reality stepped in and I pulled away, breathless.

"We can't do this."

"But your eyes are saying something different."

"It's wrong. You're married."

"But I want you. And I know you want me."

"It's the liquor talking. Go home to Jasmine and give her your love," I said, hating a woman I'd never met for possessing the man I wish I had.

He began to say something else, but stopped and released me. "Perhaps you're right; it's time to call it a night."

I nodded and he walked me over to my car. After giving me a brotherly hug, I got inside. He watched me drive away, but he didn't see the tears streaming down my face.

A couple of days later, I met Tyrone for lunch. He had already gotten a table and waved me over.

"Glad you could come."

"Hey, always glad to see you, Tyrone."

He looked down and gnawed at his bottom lip. He had a serious expression on his face when he looked at me again.

"Uh-oh, what's wrong?"

"Me. I crossed the line and I'm sorry."

"Tyrone, what are you talking about?" I asked, but knowing in my heart he meant the kiss.

"What I did the night of the Christmas Party—"

"The kiss?"

"Yes. I abused our friendship."

"By showing me what I was missing?" I said, regretting the moment it slipped out of my mouth.

A small smile appeared on his face. He had caught the significance behind it. I tried to cover it up, but I'm afraid I only made it worse.

"Just think, if you weren't married, I'd be all over you—damn! That's not what I wanted to say."

Frustrated with myself, I started to get up, but Tyrone grabbed my arm.

"Please don't go."

"I'm afraid I just made a total idiot of myself."

"No, you didn't. I have feelings for you, too. I have no idea what the future holds for me, but I certainly want to be able to count on your friendship."

I smiled despite the tears that had welled in my eyes. "I'll always be your friend, Tyrone. I promise."

"Good. Here comes the waitress. Let's order. I'm starving."

From that day on, much to my secret displeasure, Tyrone kept his word. Every

hug or kiss was platonic. We continued to emailed one another and meet for lunch. But nothing ever truly remains the same.

I hadn't heard from Takesha for nearly a week. She finally called after my umpteenth message, just as I was just about to drive over to her place to make sure she was still breathing.

"Hey, Vanessa, you called?"

"So you haven't forgotten my name and number, after all."

"Afraid I'd written you out of my will?"

"Very funny. I was concerned."

"No need to be. I've been busy. Sorry, I didn't touch base."

"With Wesley?"

"He's history. Got a new main man, James. He's from the mailroom."

"Girl, do you intend to work your way through that entire office?"

"If I have to. It's a tough job looking for Mr. Right these days. So how are you doing, girlfriend?"

"Hanging in there."

"Well, you may not have to dangle too much longer."

"What's that supposed to mean?"

"Chances are Tyrone is gonna kill his old lady."

"You are being sarcastic, I hope."

"Not really, especially after what she's been pulling."

"I'm listening." I was more concerned with what it was and how it affected Tyrone than anything else.

"Remember how she couldn't be bothered getting a babysitter so she could go to the Christmas party with Tyrone?"

"Yeah."

"Well, it seems she did hire a sitter, after all."

"For what?"

"So she could attend a more intimate party."

"Whoa! Without Tyrone?"

"Especially without him. It turns out that a few of the guys from our party left and went to the Cat's Lounge over on Fifth. Guess who they saw giving some guy a lap dance?"

"Jasmine?"

"Give that lady a prize!"

"Oh, boy. Does Tyrone know?"

"Aside from going home and most likely finding the sitter, the gossip went around the office like wildfire."

"The poor guy."

"Yeah, and it's probably not the first or last time."

"Still, there's no place for me in his life until he's got a divorce decree."

"Well, that might not be so far down the road at this point."

I shook my head. "I don't know. He won't leave Malika."

"Who says that he has to? He could win custody, you know."

"He might not still go for it. It's a major thing."

"If he has incentive, like someone special in the wings, who knows?"

Long after we hung up, Takesha's words echoed in my mind. Yet, I had a sinking feeling that Tyrone might not want to put Malika through the trauma of a divorce. And I certainly didn't help my cause much, either.

Tyrone emailed me a day later asking me to meet him for lunch on Wednesday. I of course emailed him back that I would. When I saw him at the diner, he looked tired. There was no way I could miss those dark circles under his eyes.

Halfway through the meal he asked if I'd like to accompany him and Malika to a petting zoo.

"Don't tell me that Jasmine hates animals, too."

He nodded.

"I love animals and would love to come along. When is it?"

"This Saturday."

"Ooh, that's too bad. I have a prior engagement. Maybe some other time?"

A curtain of cold air dropped as his face darkened. "Yeah, sure."

He probably didn't think I wanted to go in the first place, but I really did have a lunch date. I would go next time—that is, if there was a next time.

A few days later, I was reading in bed when the phone rang. Glancing at the time, I knew it had to be a wrong number or an emergency. I picked up the receiver and could hardly hear Tyrone's frantic voice over Malika's screaming.

"What's wrong with Malika?"

"I don't know. I can't get her to stop crying."

"Where's Jasmine?"

"Who the hell knows? Please come."

"I'll be right over."

I threw a trench coat over my nightie and grabbed my purse and car keys. I drove like a maniac and took the first parking spot I could find. Malika was still hysterical when I got there.

"Thank goodness you're here," Tyrone said. The poor guy looked so frazzled.

"Where is she?"

Hearing my voice, Malika rushed into my arms. I guess she missed her mother.

"What's wrong, baby?" I asked.

She pointed to her belly.

"Do you have to go to the bathroom?"

"I don't know."

"Why don't we try to go to the bathroom?"

"Come with me."

"Of course," I said and took her hand.

She gave it a try and jumped off the seat quickly.

"You've got to sit there a little while, honey."

"Tell me a story about a prince and a princess."

I began to tell her a story and as I was finishing, I saw a look of relief cross her sweet little face.

"Do you feel better now?"

She nodded.

"Good enough to go to sleep?"

"Will you tuck me in?"

"Of course."

After I covered and kissed her good night, I went into the living where Tyrone was nursing a beer. He saw me and immediately asked, "Is she all right?"

"She'll be fine. I tucked her in. You can go kiss her good night."

I followed him back into Malika's room. She had fallen asleep, already. He bent down and kissed her and we both tiptoed out.

119

"How can I ever thank you for coming over?"

"No need. That's what friends are for," I replied.

His eyes had fallen on what I was wearing under my trench coat. I forgot that I had opened it while I was in the bathroom with Malika and began to close it. "I should be going before Jasmine gets home."

"You don't have to worry about that. She doesn't usually crawl in until nearly dawn."

"I think I should leave, anyway. It's late and we both have to get up for work tomorrow."

"Please stay and talk to me a while. I really hate being alone every night."

I nodded.

"Would you like some coffee? I have decaf."

I shook my head. I'm fine, thanks."

We sat down on the sofa.

"You look so tired. Haven't you been sleeping well?" I asked.

"Not really. I've been so miserable."

"What's wrong, Tyrone?"

For the first time, he really confided in me. He told me how Jasmine tricked him into marriage by getting pregnant because she thought he had money. He doubted she ever loved anyone but herself. Finally, he finished by telling me about Jasmine's infidelities.

"I can't even remember the last time we had sex."

'Why do you stay with her?"

"Because of Malika."

"Sue her for custody."

"What if I lose? I can't risk it. She already told me that she'll never grant me a divorce."

"But why?"

"She's a total bitch. I've given her everything I could. I really tried to make things work."

"Perhaps, that's why. She has her freedom and security as well."

"I don't care about her, anymore. I'm in love with you."

The words hit me with the power of a rocket.

"I really should be going."

"Look me in the eyes and tell me that you don't love me."

"I can't stay…"

But his mouth was already devouring mine. I pulled away. "We shouldn't—we mustn't…"

But Tyrone either didn't hear my protests or care. Instead he moaned my name into my hair as his hands gently caressed my face and neck. I could no longer resist as his lips sought mine once more. He slipped his hand into my coat and fondled my breast through the flimsy fabric of my nightie. I could feel my nipple harden as he gently kneaded it. My moans drowned out the small voice in my head pleading with me to stop. Tyrone pushed the trench coat off my shoulders and I slipped out of it. Then he worked the nightie over my head and looked at me. "So beautiful," he murmured as he began kissing the rising swells of my breasts before lowering his mouth to suckle each one in turn. I was so lost, for I wanted that man so.

As Tyrone pulled me closer and I felt his hardness against me, I whispered breathlessly, "What about Jasmine?"

"She won't be home for hours," he said as he swept me off my feet and carried me into the bedroom, where he put me down on the bed.

I watched as he stepped out of his jeans. His manhood, thick and large, was ready for me. I don't know how many times I had fantasized about this moment and now it was actually coming true.

I took his hand and pulled him down to me. His lips captured mine and his tongue made love to my mouth leaving me breathless as he parted my thighs and gently inserted two fingers. I rubbed against his fingers and moaned once more. I desperately needed to have him inside me.

As if reading my mind, Tyrone nudged the gentle folds of my sex open with his manhood and slid all the way in. I gasped as he completely filled me. Our bodies began to move in unison. We never heard the front door open.

Jasmine had come home earlier than usual. It wasn't until she snapped a few pictures of us in bed that we realized she was leering at us.

"Get out of my bed, 'ho."

"You should talk," Tyrone spat back at her.

I was mortified and pulled the blanket off the bed, wrapping myself in it. Grabbing my things, I rushed into the bathroom. I couldn't help but hear the screaming match going on between the two of them. It was a wonder they didn't wake Malika.

"Finally caught you with your 'ho."

"She's got more style and dignity than you'll ever have."

"I'm leaving you."

"Not with this you're not. Dare divorce me and these pictures will burn you. Besides, you'll never get child custody. You might as well kiss your precious daughter good bye."

"When did you become so nasty, Jasmine?"

"Nasty? You ain't seen nothing yet, bro. I'm going out. You can tell your 'ho to come out."

I waited a few minutes before I opened the door. Tyrone was sitting on the bed; his head was between his hands. He looked up when he heard me.

"I'm so sorry, Vanessa."

"No more than I am. But, I can assure you that this will never happen again." With that, I fled from the apartment. I blamed myself for breaking my own cardinal rule of not getting involved with married men. I let my heart and emotions cloud my judgment.

After that horror show, a week passed without hearing from Tyrone. I emailed him, but got no response. I dared not call him, so I asked Takesha what was going on.

"He hasn't gotten in touch with you?"

"No. It was as if he fell off the edge of the earth. Have you seen him?"

"Very little. He's in one day, but out the next. If he doesn't pull himself together, he's going to get canned."

"Is he drinking?"

"It's possible, but the salesmen sometimes wine and dine prospective clients."

I was suddenly terribly afraid for Tyrone. More than anything, I feared that he'd have an auto accident.

After not hearing from him for almost three weeks, he suddenly showed up at my apartment one night. When I opened the door and saw him standing there, I was so filled with relief that I threw my arms around him, hugging and kissing him. "Oh, baby, I thought you were lying dead in a ditch somewhere." Then I realized what I had done.

Tyrone was grinning from ear to ear. "You do love me, don't you?"

"With all my heart and soul."

"That's what I want to hear. I'm divorcing Jasmine. I'll not have her blackmail me out of my future happiness."

"Jasmine's a fool. But, what about Malika?"

"I intend to fight for her."

I could feel my pulse racing.

"Will you marry me after I get my divorce?"

"Yes."

"Then with you by my side, how could I possibly lose?" he said as he took me in his arms and kissed me.

THE END

RUNAWAY BRIDE

"**I** know the perfect guy for you, Andrea," Shawn said. "His name is Charles, and he's dying to meet a beautiful woman."

I looked at him in disbelief. Shawn had asked me to meet him for pizza, and all he'd wanted to do was pump me for information about my best friend Linda. Fixing me up with his friend appeared to be his payment for information I had on my friend. Shawn had to be blind not to see how I felt about him.

"Well?" he persisted. "Do you wanna meet him or not?"

"Well, I guess so," I said, not knowing what else to say, considering the circumstances.

"It's the least I can do for you after all the help you've given me. Thanks a lot. Linda is the kind of girl I can fall in love with."

I loved Shawn so much I ached inside. But he wanted Linda. I couldn't very well stand in the way of way of a man determined to get what he wanted, could I?

Linda was one of those women all the guys thought they wanted but decided they didn't after they had her. Although she was a wonderful friend to me, I knew she was high maintenance for a guy. She was expensive, and she required more attention than any man was willing to give. Her relationship with Shawn lasted less than a month.

Charles had called me the night after Shawn and I met for pizza. He told me he'd heard wonderful things about me and that I sounded like his kind of woman.

"Can we get together soon?" he asked. "Like maybe this Friday night?"

"Uh, sure," I said. "I suppose we can."

"Fine. I'll pick you up at seven-thirty. That is, if it's okay with you."

"Seven-thirty is fine."

"Any place in particular you'd like to go?" he asked.

"Not really."

"Any movies you'd like to see? Favorite restaurant?"

I could tell he was eager to please me, so I thought fast. "There is one movie I haven't seen yet, and it's around the corner from my favorite Thai restaurant."

"Perfect," he said. "I've always wanted to try Thai food."

Charles picked me up at my apartment, and I was pleased that he was so cute. He wasn't quite as big as Shawn, but he had a nice, strong, athletic build. He wore his hair cut very short, and he had a big ready smile that showed a sense of humor.

From the moment we first met, I found myself laughing at Charles's jokes. And the more I laughed the more he told.

"I love Thai food," he said as he pushed his empty plate back. "I can't believe I've never tried it before. Thanks for telling me about this place."

"I've liked it ever since I first tried it, too," I said.

"And that movie," he added. "That's the funniest movie I think I've ever seen."

Charles was so sweet, I agreed to go out with him again. As he stood at my door, he told me, "I'm glad Shawn introduced us, Andrea. I've never had such a wonderful first date."

"I had a nice time, too," I told him.

Then with a chuckle, he added, "I'm just surprised he didn't keep you for himself. Shawn's a player, ya know."

"He is?" I asked.

"Yeah," he said. "That guy has more women than any other person I know. He has to write their names down so he doesn't forget them."

"Really?" I'd known Shawn for a long time. I was aware he always had a new girlfriend, but I never thought of him as a player. Now, I saw him in a completely different light.

"He must think of you as a really close friend if he hasn't put moves on you, Andrea. In my book that says a lot for you."

"Thanks for the nice evening," I told him.

He leaned down and gave me a quick kiss on the cheek. I backed into my apartment and flopped down on the sofa. To think I'd been so attracted to Shawn. He really had me fooled when he looked at me like I was special. I should have known, though, because he'd never actually asked me out on a date.

Charles and I went out several more times before we got really intimate. Sure, I found him attractive, but I wasn't totally hot for him.

When he did start making some moves, I wasn't able to get into it like I should. But we were getting pretty close, and I'd given him all the signs that I felt more than just friendship toward him.

"What's wrong, Andrea?" he asked. "Don't I do anything for you?"

"Of course, you do," I said. "It's just that I want our first time to be special."

Charles straightened up. "Okay, tell you what, Andrea. We'll make it very special. Dress up tomorrow night, and I'll give you the night of every woman's dreams."

He really was very sweet. "Where are we going?"

With a grin, he winked. "Just put on your best dress, honey, and you'll see."

I went out and bought a sparkly dress—a short one that was cut low in the front—in fire-engine red. When I tried it on with my black spike heels, I knew I looked good. Better than good.

As I stood in front of the mirror admiring myself, I decided that it was time to show Charles how much I appreciated him and the way he made me feel—special and prized. I wasn't going to act funny toward him or push him away.

"Andrea," he said in amazement, openly admiring me as I stood at my apartment door. "You're absolutely stunning."

"Thank you, Charles," I said flirtatiously. "You look handsome, too."

"We're gonna paint the town red, literally, since you're wearing that dress. And I have a special night planned for later, too."

Charles took me to the most exclusive restaurant for dinner, where he ordered for me. We ate lobster and had a bottle of a very fine wine that the waiter recommended. Afterwards, he took me to a night club where we were able to dance under the stars on the roof of a rotating bar. I had a wonderful evening.

"You haven't seen the best part of it yet," he said as his eyes twinkled.

"Where are we going?" I asked.

"You'll see."

He drove me several miles, where he pulled in front of the most expensive hotel in town. The valet parked his car, and he came around and let me out.

"I reserved a room with a view," he said. "But I won't be able to take my eyes off you, Andrea."

Charles made me feel like a fairy tale princess. As soon as we were behind the closed door of the room he'd rented for the night, he scooped me off my feet and carried me into a humongous bathroom. There, in the middle of the floor was a large, deep tub filled with water. There were bubbles and pads of flowers floating around. Beside the tub, there was a bucket of champagne and two glasses.

"I told you, Andrea," he said, "I wanted this to be a night to remember."

"Oh, I'll definitely remember this," I said as I walked around and took everything in.

"You wanna get in first?" he asked.

I looked at Charles, who stood there waiting for a response. Finally, I nodded. "Sure. I'll get in first, but don't keep me waiting."

He grinned right back. "Oh, don't worry, Andrea, I won't make you wait a second longer than it takes me to get out of these clothes."

Charles and I had kissed and groped each other, but we'd never made love before. After tonight, though, I knew things would be different.

125

The water felt warm and silky as I lowered myself into the hot tub. It was nice. I leaned against the side and closed my eyes as I luxuriated in the soothing bubbles and soft floral scent.

"Ready?" Charles asked.

I sighed. "Yes, I'm ready."

He slipped in beside me and reached for my hand. "I've been wanting to do this for a long time, Andrea."

"Take a bath with me?" I asked with a smile.

Charles pulled me close to him. "Yes, take a bath with you, pamper you, make you feel wonderful. I love you, Andrea. Making you happy is the most important thing in the world to me."

I smiled back at him. Charles was a good man. He was not only kind and smart, he was handsome and muscular. He didn't have an ounce of fat on his body, yet he was gentle as a lamb with me.

When he kissed me, I kissed him back. As our tongues darted in and out of each other's mouths, I heard a low moan in his throat.

Since he'd been determined to please me, I decided it was high time I did something nice for him. I reached out and touched the tip of his manhood, which stood at full attention.

"Andrea," he said in a husky voice. "You're sending me over the edge."

"I want to please you, Charles," I whispered.

As I fondled him, he cupped my breasts in both hands. The hot tub was tall enough for us to stand, but he pulled me to him, where he sat in front of one of the jets. As the water swirled around us, he nibbled at my nipples, bringing me to a place where I was ready for the next step.

I pulled him closer and tried to guide him inside me, but he held back. "Don't you want me?" I asked.

"Yes," he chuckled. "Of course I do. But I want you to want me, too."

He touched me all over, his fingers playing me from my breasts to my deepest core. As we writhed around in the hot tub, I realized that Charles was more intent on bringing me pleasure than satisfying himself. No other man would ever do that for me, I thought, so I needed to let loose and allow myself to love him.

When he finally deemed me ready, he said, "It's time, Angela. I want to be inside you."

He thrust his manhood deep inside me, moving in and out in a rhythm that brought me to climax very quickly. And as I cried out in joy, I felt his body shudder. We came together.

"Andrea," he said once we were satisfied and able to talk again. "I love you with all my heart. Will you make me the happiest man in the world and be my wife?"

I swallowed hard and looked him in the eye. What I saw was honesty, goodness, and unadulterated love. Slowly, I nodded. "Yes, Charles, I'd love to be your wife."

The next day, Charles insisted on stopping by a jewelry store on the way to take me home. "I want you to have the prettiest ring in the store, I don't care what it costs."

Charles was so kind and loving toward me, I knew I'd never find another man like him. After I chose a marquis cut two-carat diamond, he drove me home.

"I'll be glad when they get that ring sized and you can start wearing it," he said with the excitement of a child at Christmas. "I want everyone to know you and I are in love."

"You're so sweet, Charles," I told him. "You'll make a wonderful husband." I still couldn't bring myself to say I loved him.

The next several months went by in a whirlwind, making me nearly numb with my crazy schedule of planning the wedding. It would have been easy to fool myself into thinking I was really happy, but when I stopped to take a break, I realized I wasn't as thrilled about my upcoming wedding as I should have been. But it was too late to do anything about it. We'd already spent a fortune, and the invitations had been sent. I wasn't able to share my thoughts and feelings with anyone because I didn't think even my best friend Linda would understand.

When my concern really hit me hard was during one of our many engagement parties, where my gaze met Shawn's. He looked at me with curiosity, then he frowned. Several minutes later, he walked over to me and said, "You don't look happy. What's the matter, Andrea?"

I couldn't look Shawn in the eye now. His mere presence sent a thrill of excitement up my arm. I still wasn't over my infatuation with him, but I certainly couldn't let anyone else see it.

With a shrug, I moved away from him. "I dunno, Shawn. Maybe I'm coming down with something."

Shawn reached out and took my hand in his. Then he slowly lifted it to his lips and kissed the back of it. "Charles is a very lucky guy. I wish I'd kept you to myself. In fact, I think I made a huge mistake introducing the two of you."

I was so shocked, I didn't know what to say. Later on that night, I cried myself to sleep over how things were turning out.

Time went by very fast after that. Next thing I knew, I was standing in the front of the church, with Charles by my side, my maid-of-honor on one side, and Shawn on Charles's other side. I was fully aware of Shawn, and I even found myself envisioning him and Charles changing places. I blinked back a tear that had formed in my eye. My insides were knotting in anguish over the huge mistake I was about to make.

"Do you, Andrea, take this man, Charles, to be your lawful wedded husband, to love, to..." My ears rang as the preacher read the rest of the words I was supposed to agree to do once I was married to Charles, which would be in a few minutes if I didn't do something about it.

I licked my lips as I nervously glanced over at Shawn, who stood there watching me, his eyes hooded and brooding. This wedding was a mistake, I was now certain. I'd gone along with it, and now, here I was, marrying the wrong man.

"I can't do this," I said softly as I began to back away from the preacher.

Charles looked at me and gasped. "Andrea, what's wrong? Are you sick or something?"

When I opened my mouth, nothing would come out but a squeak. I lifted my dress, turned around, and fled the church. I didn't stop until I was outside and halfway down the block. Sure, I saw people staring at me, but I didn't care. I wasn't about to commit myself to marrying someone I didn't love with all my heart. Not only would I be miserable, making a commitment I couldn't keep wouldn't be fair to Charles.

"Andrea, wait up!" I heard from behind.

I nervously glanced over my shoulder and saw Shawn running after me, his muscular six-foot-something frame looking more handsome than should be legal in a tux. He was the man I wanted, not Charles. Shawn was the only guy I knew who could steal my breath away and make me quiver with desire at the mere sight of him.

"What do you think you're doing, Andrea?" he asked as he reached for my arm and yanked me to a sudden stop.

"I-I can't marry Charles," I said, tears finding their way to my eyes and running down my cheeks.

"Then why did you let it get this far?"

Shawn was towering over me, looking down into my eyes, his face showing concern. I knew I owed him, Charles, and everyone else in the church an explanation for my action.

"I couldn't go through with it," I said through choked sobs.

He reached out with his strong fingers and tilted my chin so I was looking him in the eye. "Is there something you'd like to tell me, Andrea?"

I swallowed hard and sniffled. Then I shook my head. "No," I squeaked.

Shawn tilted his own head back and let out a chuckle. "This is gonna sound really odd, I know, but I'm glad you ran out like you did."

Now he had my attention. "You are?"

"Yes," he said, looking at me with dreamy eyes that melted me to my toes. "In fact, I'm relieved. Andrea, I already told you I've been regretting introducing you to Charles."

"Do you mean that?" I said.

"Yes. And I was a fool."

"What now?"

He blew out a sigh. "Tell you what. Meet me at your place in an hour." He glanced down at my dress. "You might want to change and get into something a little less attention getting. We'll talk. You can tell me what's going on and why you did this."

I nodded. I had no idea what lay ahead for me, but I knew I needed to talk, and Shawn was offering to listen.

Fortunately, I'd taken my car to the church where I'd changed into my wedding dress, so I didn't have to ask anyone for a ride. The only thing I needed to do now was go inside and grab my purse.

I managed to sneak in the side door without anyone seeing me. I could tell everyone was in the preacher's office down the hall by the loud voices. Before anyone saw me, I got out and took off for my apartment.

It took me fifteen minutes to rip off the wedding dress and change into some comfortable slacks and a shirt. Shawn said he'd meet me in an hour, so I had a chance to think about what to tell him. Should I be honest, or should I continue to hide my feelings for him?

When the knock came at the door, I still wasn't sure what to do. I opened it and saw Shawn standing there, wearing blue jeans and a polo shirt, a bouquet of flowers in his hand.

"Here, Andrea," he said. "After what you've just been through, I figured you needed something to cheer you up."

After I put the flowers in water, Shawn and I went into the living room and had a heart to heart talk. All my reservations about telling him my feelings went out the window when he told he he'd always loved me.

"Why didn't you ever say anything?" I asked.

He shrugged. "I'm not sure. I guess I didn't think I was good enough for a woman like you."

"That's silly," I told him.

"There's another thing," he added. "You're the marrying type. I'm not."

I frowned. "What, exactly, do you mean by that, Shawn?"

"Well, I have no desire to settle down. But you're the type of woman who needs to have a man at home, taking care of her. A man who won't stray." Shawn looked at me long and hard. "I can't promise to be that man."

I swallowed the lump in my throat. "I'm not asking for promises, Shawn."

Time seemed to stand still as he reached for my hands and pulled me closer, but far enough apart to look into my eyes. There was obviously still a question between us, but I didn't care. I loved this man, and I was willing to take him any way I could have him.

"C'mere, Andrea," he finally said as he pulled me against his chest.

I shuddered as he stroked my back, then worked his hands around to the front and undid my blouse. His touches were sending me into a place I'd never been before—not with Charles or with any other man I'd made love to.

"I love you, Andrea," he whispered as his face drew closer to mine.

His lips covered my lips. As his tongue darted out and traced the insides of my mouth, I let him in. His moan was an aphrodisiac, sending me into orbit.

"Oh, Shawn," I said. "Let's go into the bedroom where we can be more comfortable."

He pulled away for a second. "Are you sure that's what you want, Andrea?"

Not wanting to waste another second, I quickly nodded. "Positive."

We undressed on the way to the bedroom, leaving a trail of clothes on the floor. The bed was standing there, as if beckoning us to use it. And we did.

It was so hot between us, I wouldn't have been surprised if a fire had erupted. His hand covered my right breast as his mouth came down on my neck, sending a shivering tremble down my side. My arms went up around his neck and his legs wedged between mine, separating them. I wrapped my legs around his waist.

Between kisses and playful nips on my neck, Shawn looked at me and told me I was beautiful. I pressed kisses on his face, his neck, and his chest.

"You're asking for trouble, Andrea," he whispered. "That kind of action deserves a reaction."

Next thing I knew, he had his hands between my thighs, touching me, gripping me in ways I'd never known in my life. His touch was firm yet light and playful at the same time. I was the one who was having a reaction.

"Now, Shawn," I begged. "Please, now."

"No, sweetheart," he said with a wicked grin. "I want this to be really special."

He continued to caress my feminine core as I kept begging for him to enter me. Finally, when I wasn't sure I could live another minute without him inside me, I felt him thrust his manhood between my legs. Both of us shuddered and sighed at the same time.

As he moved inside me, creating a smooth rhythm, I squeezed my eyes shut and thrilled in the ride. Shawn really knew how to make love to a woman. I continued to move as he moved, only stopping when we were both satisfied.

After he pulled out, he helped me to my feet. "Let's take a shower. Then we need to talk."

The shower created another opportunity for us to make love. I couldn't remember ever wanting a man like I did Shawn. When it was over, he helped me dry off, then we both got dressed.

Afterwards, we sat at the kitchen table and discussed what would probably happen. "I'm sure Charles will never want to see me again," I said.

Shawn shook his head. "That's one less friend for me to play ball with on Sunday afternoons."

"What now?" I asked.

"I have no idea," he replied. "But I do know that I love you, Andrea. Let's just take this thing one day at a time and see where it goes."

That was six months ago. Shawn and I still make love like a couple of rabbits, but I don't see him wanting to get married and live the happily-ever-after sort of life. That's okay for now. But he was right about one thing. I am the marrying kind. I want a husband, kids, and a house with pretty curtains. The realization that I may never have this with Shawn is starting to dawn on me.

It took my parents nearly a month to recover from the shock of what I'd done. They didn't speak to me right away. However, now that they've had time to think about it, they've told me they're glad I didn't go through with it, then get a divorce later.

Charles and I have only spoken long enough to settle things financially between us. Since I was the one who broke things off, I sent his ring back to him.

Even though I don't see a bright future for Shawn and me, I'm still glad I didn't marry Charles. If I had, I would have always wondered about how things could have been.

THE END

131